SCHIZO

SCHIZO

NIC SHEFF

PHILOMEL BOOKS
An Imprint of Penguin Group (USA)

PHILOMEL BOOKS
Published by the Penguin Group
Penguin Group (USA) LLC
375 Hudson Street, New York, NY 10014

USA | Canada | UK | Ireland | Australia
New Zealand | India | South Africa | China
penguin.com
A Penguin Random House Company

Library of Congress Cataloging-in-Publication Data
Sheff, Nic.   Schizo / Nic Sheff.   pages cm   Summary: A teenager recovering
from a schizophrenic breakdown is driven to the point of obsession to find his
missing younger brother and becomes wrapped up in a romance that may or may
not be the real thing. [1. Schizophrenia—Fiction. 2. Mental illness—Fiction.]
I. Title. PZ7.S541155Sc 2014 [Fic]—dc23 2013038592

Printed in the United States of America.
ISBN 978-0-399-16437-8
10 9 8 7 6 5 4 3 2 1

Edited by Kristen Pettit and Michael Green.
Design by Semadar Megged.   Text set in 10-point Life LT Std.
Crow images courtesy of iStock

to Jette . . . everything . . .

I was the walrus, but now I am John.

—John Lennon

PART ONE

I.

IT'S STARTING AGAIN.

There's a sound like an airplane descending loudly in my ear. I can't quite place it. The sweat is cold down my back. I feel my heart beat faster. My hands shake.

God, I can't take it.

I can't.

If it happens again . . .

I hold my breath, waiting.

The sound fades in and out—high-pitched, whining.

Preston and Jackie don't seem to notice.

They're on his bed together, which is really just like a futon on the floor, watching this old Billy Wilder movie.

Preston's arm is around her, and her arm is around him.

They are tangled together . . . intertwined.

3

Two separate people joined together into someone new and different, but still the same.

Not that I don't like Jackie. I mean, she's great. She's super great. And super nice.

They both are.

That's why they let me hang out with them.

'Cause, believe me, I bring nothing to the table.

I'm totally what you'd call a charity case.

They let me hang out and watch movies and play video games until finally Preston'll give me a look like, *Yo, me'n my girl need to have some sex right now.* And so then I'll leave.

And go home—back to my family's little three-bedroom house on the avenues, the opposite of Preston's palatial mansion up here near the Palace of the Legion of Honor. The house is like an old Gothic castle, paid for by the network TV show both his parents were on in the nineties. They played a couple on the show—a pair of married lawyers.

They're retired and they spend most of their time traveling.

Leaving Preston alone with no one but Olivia, the housekeeper.

And Jackie, of course.

Sometimes I like to think that Preston and Jackie are my parents. Except that Preston is such a big pothead. He has basically his own floor in his parents' house with a grow room set up in the closet.

I used to smoke, too, before it made me go crazy.

But that was more than two years ago.

I'm sixteen now, and it's been over a year since my last episode.

Only there's this shrill, piercing scream coming in and out of auditory focus.

It's happening again.

Preston picks up his intricately blown glass bong from the carpeted floor in front of him and takes a big hit, exhaling away from me and Jackie—being polite and all.

The thick gray smoke from his lungs smells sweet and pungent, and Preston says, "Goddamn." And then he coughs.

Jackie looks over at me and rolls her eyes, but in a sweet way.

Her eyes are this intense green color, so if I look into them when I'm talking, I get distracted and lose my train of thought. She has a long, angular nose and is tall and thin with dark black skin. She could be, like, a high-fashion model doing runway shows or whatever. She is lovely. If I weren't crazy maybe I could have a girl like her.

But it's not just that.

Preston is . . .

I don't even know.

He is everything.

And he has everything.

If she's like a high-fashion model, then he's like some kinda rock star. He has long hair parted down the middle and a scruffy beard and square jaw. He's tall and naturally muscular, and it's just the way he carries himself, like he doesn't care at all.

Really, he's been this way ever since I can remember—calm and collected and unconcerned.

Preston and I met back when we were both ten years old going to this summer camp down in Watsonville right after his grandmother died. He used to stay up nights talking to me about her. Preston still makes, like, this big deal about it. I didn't think I did anything that special, but I guess it meant a lot to him.

We've been best friends ever since—even though I didn't start actually going to school with him until my mom got the job working in the library at Stanyan Hill my seventh grade year. It's a private school, so otherwise we'd never have been able to afford it. My mom and dad kept talking about how much better an education I'd get at Stanyan, but all I cared about was being able to hang out with Preston more.

I watch him on the bed watching the movie. His arm is around Jackie, and he's resting his head absently on her shoulder. He's wearing a ripped hoodie over a vintage David Bowie T-shirt, sitting cross-legged, staring at the TV with a stoned innocence—smiling.

Jackie absently strokes his hair and then kisses him on the forehead.

They are so effortless together.

And then there is that noise again—buzzing, screaming—darting in and out.

I look around.

But I am sure now that this noise is not a real noise at all. This noise is my disease—nothing but corroded synapses and misfiring chemical reactions.

Just when I'd started to think things were getting back to normal again, the medication must've stopped working.

The air is thick and greasy-feeling from the pot smoke and the incense and our collective breathing.

I fumble to get a cigarette out of my pack.

"Miles, you all right?" Jackie whispers—staring like she wants to see inside of me to figure out the answer to her question.

I space out into her eyes for a second.

"W- . . . what? No. I mean, yeah, I'm fine."

"You sure?"

"Yeah," I tell her. "Totally."

But Preston's room is suddenly hot and claustrophobic-feeling, and the sweat on my skin is itching fucking bad. The shades are drawn and the windows are closed, and the only light is coming from the TV. I'm sitting on the carpeted floor next to Preston's bed, wanting to scratch my back, my arms, everywhere, but not doing it 'cause Jackie is still trying to figure out if I'm all right.

"You wanna go smoke a cigarette?" she asks me.

I pause, listening for that sound.

"Miles?"

And that's when I see it.

Right there, on Jackie's bare shoulder, there is this giant

mosquito. I watch as it hovers and lands and then sticks her and she calls out, "Ow, fuck!"

She slaps at her shoulder, squishing the thing against her so it kind of pops, leaving behind some blackish-looking guts and whatever amount of her blood it had managed to extract before getting dead.

"What?" Preston asks her, his voice hoarse. "What is it, baby?"

She wipes the blood and bits of splattered insect away with her hand. "Aw, gross, a mosquito."

Preston leans over to look. "In here?"

She laughs a little. "Uh, yeah . . . duh."

She grabs some Kleenex out of a box near the bed and wipes her hand clean, throwing the wadded-up tissue in the small black plastic trash bin.

And that's when she notices me—smiling big, rocking back and forth.

"What?" she asks, crossing her arms.

"It was a mosquito," I tell her.

She stares blankly. "And?"

I laugh and shake my head.

She keeps on staring at me.

"Are you sure you're all right?"

I go on and laugh some more.

Because, I mean, that's the fucking question, isn't it?

2.

DR. FRANKEL IS SHORT, practically a midget.

When he sits in his plush leather office chair, his legs dangle two or three inches off the ground. The ground, in this case, being some kind of Persian tapestry rug over a hardwood floor—a rug covered in patterns like abstract palm trees—a rug I've stared at and tried to decipher at least five thousand times in the last two years.

I'm not sure how my parents found this guy. Or how they're paying for him.

What I do know is that my visits have finally been cut down to twice a month—so I guess I'll be staring at that goddamn pattern a little less now, won't I?

Dr. Frankel coughs.

Besides being incredibly short, he is also incredibly fat. He has these giant bushy eyebrows and a huge nose and a gullet neck and he wears shiny tracksuits like a mobster. Really, I think the reason I stare at the carpet so much is that he's actually kind of hard to look at.

But, I mean, I guess he's a pretty good doctor. The meds I'm on right now seem to be working—and that is the point.

"Miles, my boy."

That's what he always calls me.

I'm not sure how I feel about that.

"Miles, my boy, how have things been? Better?"

He's eating baby carrots out of a bag, so I keep my eyes focused on that strangely patterned rug of his.

"Uh, I don't know."

I cross and uncross my legs.

He crunches noisily.

"The Zyprexa seems to be a winner, no?"

My eyes drift over to the built-in shelves with the rows and rows of different self-help books and things. A bunch of them he actually wrote himself—including the newest one: *Schizophrenia in the Adolescent Male: Signs, Symptoms, and Treatments.*

That's the one he wrote about me.

Well, me and these two other kids I see, separately, in the waiting room from time to time. Not that I've ever spoken to them. I've never talked to anyone else with this disease.

And, of course, I haven't read his book, either.

If I want to see other schizophrenics, I don't really have to look too far. This is San Francisco. I see 'em standing on every street corner downtown—yelling at cars and talking to shit that isn't there.

Those are my peers: the people who construct helmets out of plastic coolers and cardboard boxes, trying to keep the voices out. The people whose clothes are so black with dirt and oil, it looks like they're wearing sealskin. The people whose hair is tangled together into a nest of fleas and lice and whatever else. The people who have no homes or families or friends. The people walking down the street with their pants around their ankles, shitting as they go.

I've seen it, man. This city's full of them. My dad wrote this big article about it for the *Chronicle* a few years ago, claiming it goes back to the eighties, when Reagan cut funding for mental health programs. They were all thrown out into the street, and there they've fucking stayed.

But now, from what Dr. Frankel says, it's getting seriously more common, like, all the time. There was even another schizo kid at my school who had to go off to some institution at the beginning of last year. I never met him or anything, but, of course, everyone heard the story. Dan Compton, his name was. And I think half the kids in school probably expect me to go the same way.

I don't blame them. Some days, I expect the same thing. It scares the shit out of me even though, as Dr. Frankel keeps telling me, I'm the lucky one—the one the medication's been working for.

And, yeah, to answer the good doctor's question, Zyprexa seems all right.

I tell him that.

He chuckles.

"Good, Miles, good. Carrot?"

I glance up and look at the carrot he's holding out to me. The color is, like, bright, toxic orange. Really, it's the most vividly fucking orange carrot I've ever seen.

"Uh, no. I'm okay . . . thanks."

My eyes go back to the rug and then the bookshelf and then the rug again.

"How about the other medications? Are the side effects any more tolerable?"

I swivel around in my chair. "I don't know."

He crunches loudly, smacking his lips together. "You don't know?"

"Well," I say, "I still get hella nauseous when I take 'em all at once."

"So, maybe don't take them all at once."

I laugh. "Yeah, I know. But it's hard to remember otherwise."

He suggests I make myself a schedule, and I think that's pretty fucking obvious. I do some more swiveling while he does some more crunching.

"Plus, didn't I tell you?" I add. "My mom says her insurance won't cover 'em anymore 'cause the school, like, cut her hours or something."

His mouth turns down at the corners. "But aren't you working at that grocery store on the weekends?"

I laugh again. "Yeah, but that's, like, minimum wage. I mean, it's nothing."

He shakes his head. "Hmmm. Well, let me see what I can do, okay, Miles? You really shouldn't be worrying about these things. Your job is to get well. Let your parents be your parents. And let yourself be a kid—at least for a little while longer."

I pause for a second, cracking the knuckles on my left hand.

"I don't know," I say. "I mean, sometimes I don't even see the point of all this. It's like, what kind of life can I possibly expect to have? You think I'm gonna hold a job, get married, have a family?"

Dr. Frankel stops crunching, and I can hear the chair creak as he leans forward.

"You can do anything you want."

"Yeah, right."

"I'm serious, Miles. Your life is just beginning."

Yeah. Just beginning, I think. *But it's already over.*

My face contorts, and I wonder if maybe I shouldn't say what I'm about to say, but I go ahead and say it anyway.

"I appreciate you trying to give me hope and all. But I know what my chances are. It seems like I'd be doing everyone a favor if I could just end it, you know?"

He shakes his head again, and his gullet goes along for the

ride, flapping back and forth. I can smell something stale and sour suddenly, like maybe he forgot to put on deodorant this morning.

"Miles, are you listening to yourself? You don't think your parents would be absolutely, cataclysmically devastated to lose you?"

"Yeah, sure, of course," I tell him, averting my eyes again. "But, at least, then it would be over, all at once. The way it is now, I'm just gonna drag this fucking thing out so they can't ever move past it. You see what I'm saying?"

Dr. Frankel speaks gently. "Miles, come on, look at me."

I don't want to do it, but I'm too goddamn polite not to. I raise my head up as he leans in even closer.

"What?"

"Can you honestly tell me that your parents would *ever* be able to get over it if you took your own life?"

I close my eyes and open them.

My words come out all stuttered.

"Yeah, you're right. I'm not serious. But, Janey . . . she needs our mom and dad way more than I do. They—"

He cuts me off. "And what about you, huh? Doesn't your sister need you, too?"

I laugh again, but not 'cause anything's funny.

"She'd be better off without me. They all would. Besides, you think my parents will ever forgive me?"

He sits forward, so his face is up closer to mine.

"What do you mean? Forgive you for what?"

I feel a burning suddenly behind my eyes.

"You know. For what happened."

Dr. Frankel nods very slowly, and I can hear him sucking in air through his wide nose.

"You don't remember what we talked about?"

When I try to answer, the words don't come.

My throat swells.

I don't want to cry.

I don't want to fucking cry.

3.

THE SUN BURNED HOT and bright so the sweat ran into our eyes.

School was out.

We went to the beach—my mom, my dad, my little brother and sister, and me.

To Ocean Beach.

The sand was littered with trash and fallen trees and driftwood and broken-apart fishing boats, but still, the beach was pretty that day. The sky was clear blue, almost transparent so you could see the round perfect moon white in the midday sky.

The cliffs stretched up on either side.

There was no wind.

A group of surfers paddled out past the breakers—the swells forming neat, perfect lines nearly a mile out from shore.

The ocean reflecting the sky.

The ocean like a fire.

People watching the ocean like that, lying on their beach towels.

Teddy was seven then.

He was small—frail—with a whole mess of freckles and red, curly hair.

We went out wading in the water, which was cold and burned like a fire would. But the more we ran, the less it burned. And so we ran, chasing each other until I had to pee and so I went back over to my dad and Jane, who is two years older than Teddy. They were throwing a Nerf football back and forth on the hot sand—Janey with her long white-blond hair and my dad with his shirt off and his big belly hanging out over the waistband of his shorts.

When I reached the place where they'd set up camp my mom waved me over, but I ignored her and continued on toward the public bathrooms. I ran through the sand and climbed the crumbling concrete steps, up the breaker wall where a bunch of kids I recognized from my school were standing around. They were older, though, like, juniors or something—three boys and two girls. And they were smoking a blunt.

I'd smoked weed a few times before, and so I went over and they thought it was cool—some incoming freshman wanting to smoke pot with them.

The one girl, Angela, she had long dreads tucked away in a

knit Rastafarian-looking hat. And then there was Pierre, who was short and a little heavy, and then Heroji, whose father was a famous Black Panther. I'd actually met them before at the end-of-the-year picnic; they'd all been playing in the Stanyan Hill funk band, and I'd been hoping to try to audition on guitar for them once I started in the upper school.

Heroji was the one who passed me the blunt. I inhaled it deep in my lungs and held it in and then exhaled.

At the time, it really didn't seem like a big deal. I mean, like I said, I'd smoked pot before, and it wasn't like my parents would be able to see me, since we were well hidden—and the spot where they'd set up camp was a good quarter mile down the beach.

So I hit the blunt again and exhaled and I passed it back, thanking all three of them. Heroji and I did a sort of slap, snap, handshake thing, and then I ran across the parking lot to the bathroom.

I peed for a long time facing the dull-colored wall.

And then . . .

It was as though someone was there, next to me, speaking, almost whispering in my ear.

The voice was like my voice, but deeper, more grown-up sounding.

It was like my adult voice, telling me not to go back outside. *"Don't go, Miles. It's not safe. They're coming. Don't go!"*

I laughed at that.

I laughed and wondered how those couple of hits could've gotten me so goddamn high.

I walked to the door of the bathroom.

Reaching out for the handle, I tried to turn the lock, but it was like my hand couldn't quite grab hold of it.

I turned, and everything—the door, the walls, the scratched mirror, the sink, the urinals—was all covered in some kind of thick grease—like congealed fat, like wax, like Vaseline—pooling sweat, and beading in the heat of the tiny bathroom. I grabbed the handle, and my hand slipped. I called for help, but the voice was there again, telling me not to go out.

"They're coming for you, Miles. You can't go out there."

But I had to.

I had to get out.

I pounded on the door.

I screamed and screamed.

"HELP! PLEASE! HELP ME!"

But no one came.

There was only the voice.

And that's when I saw them: the crows—black, fat, grotesque, the biggest I'd ever seen—trying to break in from all sides through the sealed plastic windows and vent openings. They cawed and cackled, and I knew that the voice was right. I couldn't leave. I had to stay locked inside or the crows . . . they were going to tear me apart.

I lay on the ground and held the palms of my hands pressed

against my ears. I screamed and screamed as they clawed and cawed and fought to get in.

Honestly, I'm not sure how long I stayed there curled up on the cold gray concrete floor, or who first heard me screaming in terror, but no one could get the door open, so the fire department had to come and break through the lock with an ax.

Of course, I thought the firemen were the crows coming to take me, so I screamed even louder when I saw them and tried to run and I had to be tied down and then sedated.

It was an entire day later that I came to in the hospital.

I woke up and the doctor explained my diagnosis—starting me on my first round of medications.

They kept me on lockdown for another seventy-two hours, until finally my mom and dad brought me home.

And it was only then, over four days later, that I found out about Teddy.

No one had been watching him while I was screaming for help locked in the bathroom.

No one had been watching . . . and no one knew what happened.

When the police arrived, they found a witness who told them she'd seen a boy fitting Teddy's description getting into a Ford Explorer with a middle-aged white man—tall and thin and balding. An Amber Alert was immediately issued. They posted flyers and ran advertisements.

A few other people came forward as witnesses, too.

And there were many false leads.

But no real evidence ever surfaced as to Teddy's where-abouts.

He had disappeared.

But, of course, there was also the other possibility.

I mean, I hated to even let myself think about it, but the fact remained that the witness could have been wrong.

Maybe the boy she saw was not Teddy.

After all, Teddy had been out playing in the ocean by himself. The undertow, combined with a heavy riptide, could've easily been too strong for him.

He could have been pulled out to sea.

But I refuse to believe that.

After all, his body was never found.

And the cops and Coast Guard agreed it should have washed up on shore by now.

Teddy had to be out there.

Somewhere.

He'd be nine years old now.

It wasn't completely unheard of. Just look at that Elizabeth Smart girl. She was missing almost ten months before they rescued her.

Teddy could've been taken like that.

I have this sense that he's alive somehow. I'm not sure how to explain it. I just *feel* him—like he's not that far away at all.

Even if everyone else has given up hope.

My mom, my dad, the police, the private investigator—they've all stopped looking for him. They assume he died that day, I guess, or has died since.

But me? I can't stop looking; I can't give up hope.

Because it was my fault.

It was all . . .

All of it . . .

My fault.

So what fucking choice do I have?

4.

DR. FRANKEL LEANS FORWARD again, resting his
meaty elbows on his short legs.

"Well?" he asks, clapping his hands together. "Are you still
fixated on that day at the beach?"

I breathe out long and slow and go on, fighting back the
tears.

"I don't know," I lie. "I guess not."

"Miles. I can't help you if you don't talk to me. The medication can only do so much."

He frowns then. The clock tick-ticks on the table next to
him.

"I think maybe we should try upping the Abilify then, along
with the Zyprexa. Does that sound agreeable to you?"

"Agreeable?" I try to laugh a little, but it doesn't come out
right. "Not really—but I'll do it."

Dr. Frankel picks up the bag of carrots again.

"I promise you, Miles, you don't have to keep blaming yourself for having this disease. It is a disease, after all—completely beyond your control. You understand that, don't you?"

"Yeah. No, of course," I say.

He smiles. "And no one blames you, either."

The clock keeps on ticking.

And now all I do is wait.

5.

THE BUS GOING DOWN Geary toward our little house in Outer Richmond is an express, so it's a pretty quick trip from Laurel Village, where Dr. Frankel's office is located.

I sit on the hard, plastic, orange-painted seat. Everything smells strongly of dried sweat and some kind of hard alcohol from the homeless guy sleeping on one of the front bench seats. He's all sprawled out and drunk, which usually the bus drivers get pissed off about—though I guess they're letting it slide today.

The guy is wearing, like, five different jackets, and his sneakers are wrapped all the way up to his ankles with duct tape. He's completely passed out, his mouth open.

He could just be a regular drunk.

Or even a junkie.

But the chances are, I mean . . .

The chances are . . .

That someone like him . . . is someone like me.

Sick. Schizo. And it really only feels like a matter of time before they find me like that—sleeping in rags, riding the bus all day long 'cause I got nowhere else to go.

Just a matter of time.

I stare out the clouded window at the low-hanging fog and gray sky. We pass the Coronet movie theater and then the Alexandria.

My mom and I—we don't have much to say to each other right now, but that's one thing we still have in common.

We both love movies.

Old movies, new movies, anything, really.

For that little bit of time, I don't have to be in my head.

The only problem is, as the movie's winding down, I always get this feeling of intense sadness and dread, knowing I have to go back to my real life.

I wonder if my mom feels the same way.

In a perfect world I could just stay in bed and watch movies forever.

But I guess in that same perfect world I wouldn't have this goddamn disease in the first place.

All the kids in school wouldn't look at me like I might attack them with my pen or something—even now, two years later.

Not that the episode at the beach that day was my only one.

There was the time—a few months later—I thought Jane was trapped in the cushions of our couch. My parents walked in on me screaming and crying and tearing all the stuffing out trying to find her.

And then, just three weeks after that, at school, no less, when the crows came back, I ran screaming out of algebra class—as they clawed and pecked and tore at the doors and windows.

No one's ever looked at me quite the same since then. Not even Preston and Jackie.

People are scared, I guess.

They're scared of me.

And at home it's not much different.

The bus lurches and comes hissing to a stop as me and these two old ladies with platinum hair, speaking loudly to each other in Russian, get off at the back.

The wind is blowing strong now off the ocean, and the two old women lock arms like a married couple crossing the street together.

I walk down the uneven sidewalk—the crows circling overhead as they always do.

Whether they're real or not—delusion or reality—I have no idea.

I see them most days.

In spite of the medication they are there, among the trees and crooked branches and all along the rooftops. They duck their heads, peering out from behind the sloping rain gutters, the tapestry of telephone wires and power lines and thick, heavy Internet cables and cords connecting satellite dishes.

They live amongst the wires.

The wires that are everywhere.

Like the crows that are watching, spying, jerking their heads back, twitching, the wires are alive. Forever wrapping and tangling and tying.

Forever transmitting.

Forever receiving.

Like the fire lighting up my brain.

It is *all* schizo—the houses with their wires, the downloads and news feeds and pop-up windows.

The crows picking through the discarded waste—tearing out what's left of my, of all of our, humanity.

Everybody on earth is connected to some electronic wireless device that does nothing but create advertising and waste time and make us all ADD and ADHD and manic-depressive, neurotic, obsessive-compulsive, whatever.

I look at these houses sealed tight in all their wires—the crows waiting to come and eat what's left of our atrophied brains.

People are lighted only by the glow of their televisions or computer screens, watching the lives of other people on reality shows and YouTube videos—resentful that they themselves are not the rich and famous ones, the ones with reality shows of their own. Because somehow, in these houses with all the wires, nothing is actually worth doing unless it is seen by other people.

And so our brains turn slowly into mush.

While the crows peer and perch among the wires—waiting, biding their time 'til they can swoop in and pick clean our remains.

San Francisco is all wires and crows, surrounding me on all sides as I walk the rest of the way home. The wind sounds like someone sucking in air and swishing their tongue around in their mouth at the same time.

I pull the hood from my sweatshirt up over my head and try to protect the record that I bought at Amoeba today during our lunch break. It's an old gospel LP my dad told me about, and I'm excited to listen to it.

My mom and I have old movies. My dad and I have old music.

We both love vinyl—jazz and blues, gospel, swing, early rock and roll.

I shelter the record from the hammering wind.

And I start to run a little down the street.

The sky is nearly dark.

And the cold cuts deep inside.

6.

FOR THE PAST TEN years we've lived in a three-bedroom house in the Outer Richmond District just across from a crowded Taiwanese market that sells all kinds of cheap electronic equipment and smells of strange herbs and spices. Old women walk, bent, pushing carts, with white handkerchiefs covering their bowed heads. They wear long patchwork jackets and red-and-black sandaled clogs that tap-tap against the sidewalk and echo loudly through the streets. The men smoke brown-tipped cigarettes and shout at one another when they talk and play cards and mah-jongg on makeshift tables set up under the store's awning.

Next to the market is a bakery that makes different pastries filled with mysterious sweet and savory ingredients; my dad likes to take us there in the mornings before school. And then there's the butcher shop with links of sausage and entrails and smoked pigs' heads and whole cured ducks and chickens hanging up on display behind the large plate-glass windows. On the opposite side of the street there is a little grocery store and a Laundromat and then, on the corner, a Vietnamese restaurant, where men sit at the lunch counter eating bowls of steaming noodles and drinking beer in tall glasses. It was Teddy, actually, who liked the Vietnamese food the most. He loved anything spicy, and he'd eat the red chili paste and hot peppers straight out of the bowl, which is crazy because they make me sick as hell.

Our next-door neighbors, the Paganoffs, are an elderly Russian couple, both of them short and squat and balding. The woman wears blond wigs and white powdered makeup, and the man wears suspenders and tight undershirts that roll up at the bottom, exposing his round belly. He sits on the porch in an oversize easy chair smoking black, smelly cigars and watching his own TV through the window with the volume turned up all the way. A lot of times he'll talk to me while I'm out smoking, even though his English is terrible and I have a hard time making out what he's trying to say.

My dad buys my cigarettes for me because he figures, after everything I've been through, I should be able to smoke if I want—especially since I can't smoke pot anymore or drink or whatever 'cause of all the medication. Besides, it's only two more years until I can buy them on my own. And my dad smokes, too, so he understands where I'm coming from.

At the back of our house there is a small yard full of hard-packed dirt and tangled blackberry with nettles and artichoke. The fence is rotted out. My mom used to work out there in the garden for hours, but since that day on the beach, she's left it to grow wild.

The lot behind ours is vacant, and when I was little, I built a fort of found plywood and grocery store pallets in a clearing in the bramble. The fort was packed with sleeping bags and blankets and milk crates and comic books and flashlights. The only time I was ever brave enough to sleep out there was when I was with Eliza Lindberg, who was my best friend besides Preston in seventh and eighth grades. To tell you the truth, I was totally in love with her. I mean, it's no big fucking secret. We used to spend every weekend together, and her family took me on trips to Tahoe and even to Hawaii once.

I fell in love with her the very first time we hung out. We went to a movie after school, and Eliza bought M&M's and poured them into her popcorn, and we ate the M&M's/popcorn mixture as the chocolate melted and our hands touched in the dark.

She loved movies like I did and music and we used to talk really intensely for hours on the phone all about our families and everything. I think we were both able to tell each other things that we couldn't tell anyone else. She trusted me to keep her secrets, and for the most part, I trusted her to keep mine. She would talk to me about her dad, who was this celebrity chef, being gone all the time and her mom's drinking. And I'd tell her about my mom's crazy up-and-down moods and how I felt so different from all the kids my age—including Preston—like this alien dropped off on the planet by mistake. Not that I wasn't friends with the other kids in my class; I was. But that feeling of otherness never left me, like I could never let anyone know who I really was.

Until I met Eliza.

Because she was like an alien, too, dropped on Earth from whatever planet it was that I came from.

She was *like* me.

And we listened to music together and watched movies and slept out in that fort at night talking about school and our dreams and everything, really.

We relied on each other.

At least, we did when we were together after school. Around the other kids in our class, she would ignore me or even make fun of me sometimes. Maybe she was embarrassed because of the stuff she told me. I never could figure it out. I just had to content myself with knowing that, when we were alone together, she understood me and I understood her.

She remained my closest friend for all of seventh and eighth grades.

But then I ruined everything.

I mean, everything.

And still I can't help thinking about her—pretty near every day.

As I climb the white painted wooden steps to our house, I

wonder if maybe I should take that fort apart. But I know that's stupid. I'd just go on thinking about her whether the fort was there or not.

Across the low picket fence I see Mr. Paganoff, the Russian man next door, sitting in his easy chair, wrapped in a heavy coat against the cold. I wave to him, and he smiles very wide.

"Miles!" he announces proudly, as if maybe he'd been struggling to remember my name.

The shops across the street are all shut down for the night and there are no cars driving past, so there is only the noise from Mr. Paganoff's TV blaring as I unlock the door.

Inside there is a fire going, and one of my dad's old jazz LPs is playing on the record player.

I put my stuff down by the front door and Jane comes running over.

Jane's hair is darker now, like mine, and she wears it long and messy just like I do. Actually, I'd say of my whole family, it's Jane and I who look the most alike. Though, luckily for her, she's a whole lot prettier than I am.

"MILES!!!" she yells.

I bend down and kiss the top of her head. "What's up, little frog?"

She laughs at that. "We're making brownies."

I notice the chocolate smeared across her face. "I see that. Can I help?"

She smiles and nods. "Of course."

"Hey, I almost forgot," I tell her. "I got a new record from Amoeba. You wanna listen?"

Again she nods. "What is it?"

I grab the record from off the floor next to my bag. "Some guy Dad told me about. He's, like, an early twenties Christian gospel blues singer. He played this weird instrument called a phonoharp, I think."

She crinkles her nose. "A phonoharp?"

"That's what it says."

She takes my hand in hers. "You know, you are seriously a weirdo."

And then, when I don't answer right away, she adds, "I mean that in a good way."

"Well, thanks. And you . . ." I pause. "Are very, very normal."

She laughs some more.

Because the house is small, pretty much everything is in the front room by the fireplace. The couch is relatively new, some cheap thing my dad and I had to put together from Ikea, considering I massacred the last one. And there's a big La-Z-Boy. The floors are all hardwood and uneven, like you're walking on a ship, and the walls are painted a dull yellow color. There's a crack running jaggedly across the ceiling starting from the front door that lets in water when it rains. One of my dad's buddies came by a couple years ago with some plaster sealant, but, for whatever reason, it didn't work. Every winter the crack just grows a little deeper. There's a rust-colored stain bleeding out from the center. Even now I can see condensation forming there from the fog coming in.

It's one of those things we don't like to talk about, though. My mom gets upset whenever she sees it or thinks about it, and then she'll start picking at my dad about why he hasn't fixed it, and he'll take it and take it until he snaps back and then they have a huge fight.

When that happens it's my job to take Jane into my room and read—usually from this collection of stories we've always loved called *Nathaniel and Isabel.* They're these books that I think are French, but translated into English, about two children who've run away from an orphanage and this evil governess lady who's always after them. The stories are all pretty much the same, with the two little orphans always escaping just at the last second. But I was obsessed with those books when I was a kid. Whenever I was scared at night, I'd get up and read them to myself until I could fall back asleep.

I used to read them to Teddy, too, and Jane—and I still read them to her when our parents fight.

Which really isn't all that much, honestly. It's just that crack in the ceiling that sets my mom off. So we live beneath it without ever looking up at it.

Now, since Teddy's disappearance, we mostly just eat dinner on our laps watching TV or whatever, but tonight, for some reason, my dad's decided to cook something nice—roast pork and Brussels sprouts (which, maybe surprisingly, I love)—so he wants us all to eat at the actual dining room table.

I go over and change the record on the turntable.

All the nice stuff we have is from back when my dad still had his staff job at the *Chronicle*. The record player, the speakers, the TV, the PlayStation, the DVD player, our cell phones, the computer, even the art and photographs. It's like the whole house is frozen in some sort of time warp.

Like we're still living in 2010.

The record crackles loudly as it finds its rhythm, and a man starts in, talking.

"What are they doing in heaven today? I don't know, boy, but it's my business to stay here and sing about it."

And then he does, his voice coming through clear and pained and beautiful. Just his voice and that strange instrument, sounding like a child's toy.

"This is awesome," Janey says.

We pour the brownie mixture into a pan and then take turns licking chocolate batter off the long metal spoon.

"What is this terribly depressing music?" My mom comes out of her room wearing a plush-looking bathrobe over her loose-fitting striped pajamas. "Is this yours, Miles? Go turn that off right now."

Jane looks up proudly. "It's a phonoharp."

My mom remains unconvinced.

"I mean it, Miles. Turn it off. It's too depressing."

"Okay, okay," I say, going over to turn the record off.

She stands there for a moment, breathing.

"I'm sorry," she finally says. "I didn't mean to snap at you. I've just been so . . ." She trails off.

"It's okay," I tell her. "I get it."

She goes to take Dad's roast out of the oven, replacing it with the pan of brownie batter. She puts the roast on the stove-top and turns toward me. Her hair has gone almost completely white since Teddy's disappearance. And, while she's always been very thin, now it's like she's almost sickly. Her hands are knotted and arthritic-looking. There are lines and creases around the corners of her mouth and eyes. I don't say that to be cruel. I know it's my fault. I've made her this way.

"Hey, Mie," she starts, somewhat abruptly. "Was everything okay today? I didn't see you at lunch."

My mom works as the librarian at my high school, and ever since I got sick, I'm supposed to check in at least once a day to make her feel better. But I realize now that somehow, today, I totally forgot.

"Well, I . . . I . . ."

"He went to buy that record," Jane says.

I smile down at her. "That's right, I went to buy that record."

My mom shakes her head. "You know you're only supposed to spend your money on your cell phone . . . and to help out with your medicine now that the insurance has run out."

"That's all I do," I tell her. There's a pressure building

steadily on either side of my forehead, like the veins at my temples are filling with blood and starting to squeeze my brain underneath. "It was Dad who told me to buy the record."

"Well, he shouldn't have done that," she says. "I'll talk to your father about that later."

I close my eyes tight, and it's like there's a strobe light flashing in the darkness. My teeth grit together. The medication I'm on always gives me these terrible headaches, but somehow this feels even worse than normal.

And then I hear my dad shouting from their room.

"Talk to me about what?"

I open my eyes to see him walk out wearing pajama bottoms and a San Francisco Giants T-shirt that's a little too small for his big belly.

He looks over in my direction. "Miles. What's up, buddy?"

He comes over and messes my hair; he smells like soap and laundry detergent. His hulking frame looms over me, considering he weighs a good seventy pounds more than I do. Plus he's, like, six foot three, so he's got me beat by at least four inches. There's something comforting about his size, though, making me feel so small like it does.

"Hey, Dad," I say.

My mom tells him to sit down. "Sam, come on, dinner's ready."

Sam is my dad's name. My mom's name is Audrey. Sam and Audrey Cole. I think they were happy once.

My dad goes over to wrap his arms around her, but she pulls herself free, turning to face him.

"Did you really tell Miles he could buy a record today?"

My dad makes a face over at us, clenching his teeth together and dropping his head down so it looks like he has about five chins. Then he turns back to Mom and kisses her on the cheek, grabbing her around the waist again and shouting out, "Guilty!"

She doesn't smile. "We talked about this."

"Oh, honey, come on. He works hard for that money. Anyway, it was probably just . . ." He glances back at me. "Miles, how much did that record cost?"

"Four dollars," I say, but quietly.

"See? Only four dollars."

She squints her eyes, kind of glaring at him. "Four dollars?"

I go over to the record player, grab the sleeve off the floor, and hold it up for my mom to see.

"Four dollars," I say.

Her mouth seems to form a smile in spite of itself.

"I'll get the plates," Dad tells her, giving her a quick kiss on the forehead. "You go on and sit down. You want a drink?"

"I'll take a beer."

She comes over to the table then and sits down next to Jane.

"How 'bout you guys?" he asks. "You want some lemonade or something?"

Jane smiles. "Yes, please."

Despite the pounding in my head, I get up and go over to

the refrigerator to get the drinks for my mom and sister. I open the beer on the edge of the counter, hitting the bottle cap hard with the palm of my hand.

"Miles, don't open it like that," my mom says.

I look over at her. The skin around her mouth is all puckered and withered—her eyes are deep set with wrinkles. She has grown cold and bitter. From what she was, to what she is now . . .

It's too terrible to even think about.

How can I ever make it up to her?

How can I make it up to Jane, to my father?

How can I make it up to Teddy?

If he's alive . . .

But I know he *is* alive.

I feel it.

I feel him.

Mom, Dad, the police, the press—they may have given up on him, but I never will.

The blood seems to swell and the veins tighten around my brain. The pain cuts in.

"I'm sorry," I say.

But that isn't enough. It can never be enough.

I have to do more.

I have to make it right.

But how?

7.

THE SCHOOL AT STANYAN Hill is small, maybe a thousand kids total, built out of an old converted church and churchyard. There's a tall wrought-iron fence surrounding the entire property and an orchard of crab apple trees and cherry blossoms and an Astroturf soccer field that separates the kindergarten through eighth grade classrooms from the upper school.

The roof of the main building collapsed in a storm two years ago, so they redid the entire thing out of white stucco like one of those Spanish-style missions. They planted red roses and pink bougainvillea and a vegetable garden in the back with all kinds of lettuces and carrots and radishes they serve in the salad bar in the cafeteria.

There's a brand-new performing arts center and a theater and an indoor pool and an art studio and a science lab and

SCHIZO

an athletic center with a full gym and tennis courts. There is, however, no football field, as the school has no football team.

No football team, no basketball team, and no baseball team, either.

Not that I've ever been super into sports or anything. Still, there is something incomplete-feeling about going to a high school that doesn't offer those kinds of all-American sports. Like if our school didn't have a prom. I mean, there's no way in hell I'm going to go, but at least I get to make that decision myself. If we didn't have a prom at all, then I wouldn't be able to reject it, now would I? And what would the fun be in that?

Growing up in basically the most liberal city in the country, there aren't a whole lot of opportunities for rebellion. You have to get creative if you want anyone to notice your goddamn teenage angst.

When I think about my dad growing up in Georgia in the seventies and how much he had to rebel against, I gotta say, I'm pretty jealous.

Maybe having schizophrenia is my big fuck-you to the status quo.

Only, I guess at this point, being normal and well-adjusted would be, like, the biggest fuck-you of them all.

So I guess I'll just try to shoot for that, if I can.

Monday morning the rain falls steadily against the bus window as we lumber down Fulton past Golden Gate Park. I can see the street kids camping out in brightly colored sleeping bags and tarps laid out across the grass.

A lot of days my mom and Jane, who's still in the lower school, will come with me on the bus, but they don't have to be in 'til later this morning, so I'm alone, listening to these old Marc Bolan records on my iPod.

The bus pulls over at the corner and I get out, hurrying up the block. I have a hoodie pulled down over my eyes and I keep my headphones on while I show my ID to the guard and then run down the carpeted steps to the basement floor where our lockers are set up. The smell of sweat and mildewed, damp clothing fills the hall, and there's a bottle of Gatorade spilled on the floor beneath my locker, so my sneakers squish, squish along the carpet.

Bodies move past in all directions as I unload my books into the locker.

I have biology first period, so I hold on to my science book and calculator and a notebook, but that's about it. The music is playing loud in my ears, and I close up the locker and spin the dial on the combination lock, and then something hits against me and I turn, startled.

It's Ordell Thornton, one of the few people in this school who isn't afraid of me.

He mouths something at me that I can't hear 'cause of the music. I watch his jaw and cleft chin and coarse-looking scruff on his face moving again and I take the earphones off.

"What?"

He pushes his long dreads behind his tiny ears, which stick out practically at a perfect ninety-degree angle from his head.

"Dude, I called you, like, five times this weekend. What's up? You avoiding me or something?"

I take a step back. "Uh, no. Not at all."

He smiles real big. "I'm just playin' with you. But seriously, yo, where you been at?"

I shake my head. "Nowhere. I mean, home. I've been sick."

As much as Ordell's nice to me and all, his dumb, surfer-dude act is super annoying. I tend to lie and make up excuses so I don't have to hang out with him.

"You're always sick," he says.

He stands aside while I grab my bag from the floor, and we walk together back up the stairs to our first period classes. Ordell's another one, like Preston, who I've been going to school with since back in seventh grade.

"Dude," he says again, huffing and puffing up the stairs. "Candace had a party at her mom's house on Saturday. It was off the hook. Ian's brother brought a keg, and you know Candace's boyfriend, Taj, from Berkeley High? His dad grows weed for the dispensaries, so they had joints of this chronic-ass shit just laying out on the table like fucking party favors."

He rambles on about the party, and I keep my head down, looking at the carpet and all the different stains and dried pieces of gum and ground-in whatever. I notice a flyer for the Winter Formal tacked up near the railing, and I ask Ordell if he's bringing anyone, really just to say something.

He lowers his eyes and talks low, like he doesn't want anyone to hear.

"Yeah, man, uh . . . actually . . . I was thinking of asking Helena."

"Helena's a good choice," I say, which I guess is true considering she's pretty much as airheaded as he is.

He smiles. "What about you? You gonna ask anyone?"

I laugh at that 'cause it's so totally ridiculous.

"No," I tell him.

I take another step.

And then I stop.

And that's when I see her.

I miss the top step and fall hard onto my knee.

Thankfully she doesn't seem to notice.

She doesn't seem to see me at all.

Ordell laughs from the back of his throat. "Dude? What the fuck?"

I'm sweating now and the heat surges through my body, so I take off my jacket and pull myself up, saying, "Hey, did you see that?"

Ordell laughs some more. "Yeah, dude. Duh."

"No, man, not me."

I wonder, then, is this just another hallucination? An apparition created by misfiring synapses in my brain?

But . . . it seemed so real.

"Was that Eliza?"

Ordell narrows his eyes at me. "What?"

I swallow hard. "Was that Eliza Lindberg?"

Ordell nods. "Yeah. You didn't know she was back?"

"N-no . . . I didn't."

And then Ordell starts to laugh hard and squeezes my shoulder. "Oh, yeah, I remember. You hella liked her, right?"

"No," I say. "No, I'm just . . . I'm surprised."

"Yeah, you know her dad's, like, some big restaurant guy."

"Yeah, yeah, I know."

"So they just moved to open up that restaurant."

"In New Orleans."

"See, you knew about it."

I grab my backpack. "Yeah, I just didn't know they were back."

"Well, they are." He laughs again. "We gotta go to class, man. But seriously, call me, all right?"

He punches me in the chest so I take a step back and almost trip down the stairs again.

"Yeah, totally."

He walks off and I start down the hall past the still-life drawings hung up from the freshman art class, done in gray charcoal and pencil.

Bodies walk past me in both directions, and the lights are flickering overhead, and everything is all smudged around me like the drawings on the wall.

"Jesus Christ," I say out loud.

Eliza Lindberg.

I guess I knew she'd be coming back at some point. After all, this is her home. And setting up a restaurant in New Orleans couldn't take forever.

Two years.

I haven't spoken to her once since that last day—that day that I fucked it all up, that day that I asked her to be my girlfriend.

Like I said, it was the end of eighth grade, and I guess I was just nervous that once we started high school she was going to forget about me or something. Behind the gym after school, I asked her if she would "go out with me." She started crying and yelling at me that I'd "ruined everything," which was true, though I didn't know it at the time.

It was only a few weeks later when Preston told me she was moving with her family to New Orleans to open another one of her dad's restaurants.

I felt sick at the thought of never seeing her again.

But then, just a month after that, I had my first episode at the beach. And then I was grateful Eliza would never have to see me like that—delusional, crazy, strapped down to a hospital gurney. She would never have to know about what happened to me. She'd never have to know what I did to Teddy. That was the one good thing out of all this fucking bad.

But now I wonder . . .

Does she know?

The question repeats itself over and over in my mind, like one of my dad's old records, the needle skipping.

Does she know?

Does she know?

Because all I wanted was for her to never find out.

I push past a couple freshman boys whispering in the hall, and then I turn in to the classroom. Our biology teacher, Mr. Heinz, is a small man with chiseled features—Germanic-looking. He has blond hair parted to one side and he is very tan. He's playing a classical music CD on an old boom box splattered with white paint. Bach piano concertos. *The Well-Tempered Clavier,* Book 1 or 2. My dad has the same album on vinyl at home. The music is simple and clear and melodic.

"Take a seat, Miles," Mr. Heinz whispers. "We're solving these Punnett squares. Please try not to disturb everyone." He gestures to the whiteboard, where a complicated genetics problem has been written out in green marker.

I nod and whisper back, "Okay."

Mr. Heinz always starts his class exactly on time, so even if I'm, like, a minute late he acts like I missed half the period.

I go and take a seat next to this girl Alexis, who I know pretty well. She has black hair with bangs and bright red lipstick.

"Hey, Miles," she says very quietly.

"Hey."

My body lands heavily in the hard wooden chair. Someone

has carved the words *Roberta Blows* into our desk. I'm not sure who Roberta is.

I nudge Alexis gently to show her the carving.

"Right?" she says, smiling.

"Did you know Eliza Lindberg was back at school?" I ask her. Alexis was in our seventh and eighth grade classes, too.

"Eliza?" She narrows her eyes at me. "No. *Really?"*

And then Mr. Heinz calls out, "Solve the problem quietly, guys."

And so I put my head down. I try to do what he says.

But I'm shaking now, trembling so my writing comes out all scratchy, nearly illegible.

My mind keeps going around in circles—manic, anxious, remembering.

I feel like I might actually get sick.

My stomach seizes.

And there's sweat all down my back and broken out on my forehead.

"Hey, are you okay?" Alexis whispers.

I stand up.

"Yeah, uh . . . no . . ."

I walk quickly out of the room, ignoring Mr. Heinz calling out to me.

When I get to the bathroom, I lock myself in one of the stalls and get ready to puke.

It's just the medication, I tell myself, *eating through my stomach.*

It can't possibly have anything to do with Eliza being back.

I think about Mr. Heinz and the Punnett squares—dominant and recessive traits. But where this fucking mental illness comes from, I have no idea. No one else in my family is crazy like I am. I'm the defective one—the mistake. And I am obviously not fit for survival. If I were out in the wild, I would've been left for dead long ago.

I curl up as small as possible on the floor and wait for the nausea to pass.

8.

THE LIBRARY AT STANYAN Hill is pretty unimpressive for a private school.

It's about the size of two classrooms put together, the shelves filled with big reference volumes no one ever looks at and a whole lot of paperback teen fiction like the *Twilight* series. There are a few classics and some oversize collections of poetry and short stories. And then there is a whole wall of different magazines.

My mom has been fighting for years to get them to expand the library, or at least to expand their collection, but it's never been a priority. From what I've seen, the library is just kind of an afterthought. The school spent all this money building a big fancy computer lab and stocking it full of brand-new Macs, so barely anyone even uses the library anymore. In a lot of ways,

I'm surprised my mom still has a job here. The library is pretty much empty every time I go in.

And today at lunch is no exception.

The door is propped open and my mom is sitting on a stool behind the desk reading a book herself. There are a couple of freshmen reading a graphic novel together at one of the round wooden tables in the corner by the window. They are very small and very young-looking, with pasty, pale skin. They have on preppy sweaters and loose-fitting jeans and white old-man sneakers. They are dorks. They part their hair on the sides. They hang out in the library during lunch.

But then again, so do I.

"Hey, Mom," I say, startling her from whatever book she's reading.

"Shhhh," she tells me, holding a finger up. She's wearing a thick wool sweater and a knit scarf and her librarian glasses. Her hair is cut a few inches above her shoulders.

I look over at the two nerdy freshmen again and raise my shoulder up, like, *Seriously, I have to be quiet for these guys?*

She follows my gaze and then smiles and gestures for me to go back into her office. I follow her along the thick carpeting that still smells new all throughout this floor of the school.

Her office is small, about the size of a closet, with a desk and no computer and a couch my mom brought in herself from Goodwill. She has pictures of me and Jane and Dad up on the wall. There're even a couple pictures of our cat, Myshkin. But there are no pictures of Teddy—just as there are no pictures of Teddy in our house.

I can't blame her.

Remembering is painful.

But, pictures or no pictures, I'm sure he's with her every second, the way he is with me.

His picture is projected there on the backs of our eyelids.

So we don't need it hanging in a frame.

I take a seat on the shiny upholstery, and the springs whine and buckle beneath my not-very-substantial frame. My mom sits in her broken office chair that's been stuck in the lowest position to the ground, so she appears very short, even though she's a whole inch taller than I am.

"Here you go," she says, handing me a plastic-wrapped peanut butter sandwich and a small, roughly textured apple. "Would you like some coffee?"

The lines and creases around her mouth are deep set so that when she purses her lips together it gives the appearance of a dried-up piece of fruit.

I nod yes.

She pours black, bitter-smelling coffee from out of the large stainless steel Thermos into a metal camping mug and passes it over. I take a bite of the sandwich made on processed wheat bread with strawberry jelly that leaks out the side. I wipe my mouth on the sleeve of my undershirt.

"Thanks," I say.

She drinks her coffee but does not eat.

"Mom," I start hesitantly, looking down at the scuffed-up toes of my boots. "Mom . . . did you . . . uh . . . did you know Eliza Lindberg was back in school?"

My mom freezes up, the coffee mug held just inches from her open mouth.

"No . . . I didn't."

She completes the sip of coffee, and I take a bite of sandwich, talking with my mouth full.

"Yeah. I saw her. I guess they're back from opening that restaurant in New Orleans."

My mom sets the coffee down and leans forward, intertwining her fingers on her crossed knees. Her eyes narrow behind her horn-rimmed glasses.

"Miles, I promise, I had no idea. I would have told you."

"No, no, I know. I didn't mean it like that."

"Well, are you gonna be okay? Have you talked to her yet?"

"No, I haven't. But, uh, yeah, of course I'll be all right. It's just weird, is all."

My mother stares like she's trying to see something hidden inside me. I stay quiet.

"Well, just be careful, Miles."

I laugh, then, at that—though, of course, I know she's right. Even before Eliza rejected me straight out, I was always getting messed up about her. There was this one time when we were on a class ski trip that all us kids were playing Truth or Dare up in the girls' bunks in the lodge. Someone dared Eliza to kiss me, and she acted like just the thought of it was the most disgusting thing in the world. She told everyone it made her want to barf. So she never did kiss me on the dare, and I was so crushed, like my insides had all been torn out of me.

But then, the next day when we found ourselves alone on the ski slope, she came up to me and kissed me very quickly on the mouth. She whispered that she was just completing her dare. Then she skied off. And, of course, I was fucking elated. It's lame, to say it like that, I guess, but I don't care. I *was* elated. And I thought for sure it meant she liked me.

Of course, it wasn't too long after that she was back being mean to me in front of everyone again.

"Yeah," I say. "I mean, no, you're right."

My mom sits up a little straighter. She takes a sip of her coffee and then leans forward even closer this time.

"I'm serious, Miles."

"Yeah, so am I," I tell her. I look up at my mom's weathered face. "You don't have to worry."

I take another bite of sandwich. That is the truth. Only I don't know how to explain it to my mom so she'll understand.

How could I ever let myself get involved in any kind of romantic relationship when Teddy is still out there, missing, and it is my fault? How could I ever let myself have any kind of happiness?

No, until Teddy is found, I'll never be able to move on with my own life.

None of us will.

Our whole family is trapped in a state of perpetual suspended animation.

We are frozen, waiting.

And what will save us? What will allow us to start living again?

Finding Teddy.

That is all.

My mom sips her coffee.

And that's when it hits me.

Something has to be done.

And I think, for the first time, that I'm the one who has to do it.

Teddy is out there. It's up to me to bring him home.

There's a voice whispering through my mind—like sunlight shining in, like the ocean swelling around me, like the world has broken wide-open and I am standing at the very center of the universe.

I am the one.

I have to find him.

And I will.

9.

OUR JUNIOR CLASS IS a lot bigger than our grade school class used to be, but it's still super small compared with most high schools, and there really isn't any way to avoid running into someone you don't want to see.

Inexplicably, though, I managed to make it through two whole days before seeing Eliza again.

But today we're having a whole-school assembly, so I know I won't be able to avoid it.

We all file in together to the newly remodeled auditorium. I sit next to Preston and Jackie, but they're busy looking meaningfully into each other's eyes, so they don't even seem to notice me as I scan the room—looking for Eliza.

And then I see her.

She walks in by herself.

Her hair is even darker than I remember, black and full and layered. She's wearing ripped jeans tucked into calf-length boots, a gray cardigan sweater, and a loose-fitting T-shirt. She is tall and thin and beautiful.

I watch as she takes a seat at the front, seemingly oblivious to the rest of the herd moving past her. Preston leans in close to me.

"Dude, stare much?"

I'm startled a little by his sudden attention.

"What? I'm not staring at anyone."

He laughs. "Yeah, right."

I breathe and hold the air in my lungs before exhaling all at once as I ask him, "Well, have you talked to her?"

"Uh, yeah," he says, averting his eyes. "I did real quick. Sorry, man, I couldn't help it."

My stomach knots up, and I keep glancing down at the place where Eliza is sitting. It really does seem like the more you try not to think about something, the more that ends up being the only fucking thing you *can* think about. That's the way it is with Eliza. In spite of myself, and all my intentions, I can't help but want to know.

"Did she ask about me?"

Preston coughs and looks over at Jackie. "Yeah, a little."

"What did she say?"

"I don't know, man. She asked about you."

"Really?"

"Yeah, it seems like she maybe wants to apologize or something. Like she realized how fucked up she was being to you."

Great, I think, *so she feels sorry for me. That's exactly what I fucking need.* But what I say is, "Nah, man, she doesn't need to do that."

Preston shakes his head. "Hell yes, she does. But if I were you, I might give it some time. I don't want anything . . . you know . . . bad to happen."

There's a heat swelling in my brain. I wish that everyone would stop worrying about me. I'm not some total invalid.

But what I say is, "Of course, man. Forget it. I really don't care."

He laughs then. "Sure."

"I don't," I tell him. "I've got more important things to do than worry about Eliza Lindberg."

"Yeah? Like what?" he asks.

"I just . . ."

"What?"

"I . . ."

But I don't try to explain. I can't tell Preston what I'm planning to do—what I've been chosen to do. I can't tell anyone. They wouldn't understand. They'd tell me I was wasting my time, that I was getting in over my head, that I was being stupid, naive, and whatever else.

And, hell, maybe I am.

But it doesn't matter.

Preston smiles again as he says, "Well, anyway, that party I'm having Saturday night? Eliza told me she's gonna be there. And, uh . . ." He pauses, looking back at Jackie, before continuing on. "She did say she wanted to see you."

My face goes flush then, and there's this tightening in my stomach.

"She wants to see me?"

Preston nods slowly. "So that means you're coming then, huh?"

I force myself to breathe. "No, man, I told you, I don't care about Eliza."

"So you're *not* coming?"

"I don't know, man. I'll see."

He leans over to Jackie. "He's totally coming."

She laughs, her white teeth flashing. "Please come," she says to me. "At least I'll have someone to talk to. I hate his big parties."

"Me too," I tell her.

Preston sets his jaw, then click-clicks it back and forth. "Well, no one's forcing you all."

Jackie kisses him quickly on the cheek. "No, I'll be there. You should come, too, Miles. We can hide out in Pres's room together."

I nod, suddenly distracted—listening to the mass of students talking at once, the sound like the steady vibrating hum of a working beehive, growing ever louder, as though someone has come along and shaken the thing up, the drones swarming, agitated, driven blindly by some unknown desire.

And there is Eliza.

She is sitting there, silently, in the very center.

As if it were all for her.

And so I tell myself, again, that finding Teddy is all that matters.

Preston's party.

Jackie.

Eliza.

Goddamn school assemblies.

The swarming hive.

None of it matters.

It is all meaningless.

"Anyway," Jackie continues, "there'll be so many people, you probably won't even see Eliza."

"Yeah, that's true."

Our school principal, Ms. Brizendine, steps up behind the podium on the stage.

The noise of the swarm starts to quiet down around us.

Eliza sits very still.

And I try not to notice.

10.

IF THERE'S ONE THING I've learned from watching all those film noirs with my mom, it's that detectives always begin by interviewing the primary witness. And, in this instance, Dotty Peterson is not just the primary witness, she is the *only* witness—the one who told the police she saw Teddy getting into that truck.

I've never actually met Dotty Peterson, myself—considering I was in the hospital the first seventy-two hours after Teddy's disappearance—but her name, along with the town she lived in, was printed in pretty near every article there was on the kidnapping at that time.

So finding her, these two years later, was actually super easy. All I had to do was call information. She was listed as D. Peterson of Burlingame, California. The operator connected me, and Dotty answered on the second ring.

Of course, I was nervous as hell, calling her like that—my voice shaking all over the place as I tried to explain who I was and what I wanted—but she was very nice and very patient. She even agreed to let me go to her house to talk about Teddy and to have, as she put it, "a good chat." She told me several times how sorry she was for me. She really was very nice.

It's only a short bus ride down to Burlingame, so after work, I go to catch the Muni over on 19th Avenue. It takes a while for the bus to get here, but I finally see it coming through the fog, rattling loudly, then stopping with a hiss of its breaks.

The bus driver, a tall, heavily built man with a gray coarse-looking beard, glances without interest at my bus pass. The whole bus is pretty near empty. There's a man wearing a tattered corduroy three-piece suit that looks at least thirty years old. That is, the suit looks that old; the man looks much older. He rubs his chin with his thumb and forefinger over and over and seems to be speaking silently to himself, repeating words like he repeats the motion of his fingers.

Another man, also in his fifties—or even sixties, I'd say—with a big white beard and his hair slicked back, stares straight down at his own hands, which are twisting and tightening around themselves.

There is a small woman with a thick down jacket and a clear plastic bag covering her hair, presumably to protect it from the moisture in the air outside.

I sit at the back on the hard plastic seat and take out the

book I'm supposed to be reading for school—Leo Tolstoy's *War and Peace.* It's a big fucking thing to carry around, but I don't mind because I really do love it—only, right now, I can't seem to focus. My eyes are blurred, my thoughts scattered. I read three whole pages before I realize I haven't remembered or comprehended a thing.

Outside, along the rows of white two-story Victorian houses, the soft glow of Christmas tree lights blurs past in the front bay windows. The sidewalks are deserted, though there's a steady stream of traffic on the street. The bus lurches and stops, and the driver honks impatiently at a truck stalled in our lane.

There are well-fed but idle-looking black crows lazily grooming themselves, perched high up on the dead trees in the center island.

The crows line the telephone wires, the rain gutters, and the rooftops.

Crows everywhere.

Again.

Always.

Forever reminding me that I am on the edge—teetering—fighting to hold on to the real through the unreal.

Teddy.

He is what's real.

My nine-year-old brother—out there somewhere, terrified and alone.

Finding him is all that matters.

I watch the fog beginning to dissipate as we climb out of the avenues, turning right past San Francisco State, merging onto the 101 Freeway.

It ends up taking about half an hour to get to the bus stop closest to where Dotty Peterson lives. Burlingame is all suburban developments and strip malls and wholesale markets.

The sky is clear and cold. I pull my hood down low over my eyes, walking up a residential street of run-down houses, mostly surrounded by chain-link fencing and rock gardens. A blue-gray, shaggy, medium-size dog comes running up from one of the yards. His bark is high-pitched as he jumps at the fence.

A few cars drive slowly past. There's a pair of ragged-looking squirrels chasing each other up a barren fruit tree. The blue-gray dog notices the squirrels and goes off after them, spinning in little circles at the corner of the fence. It barks and barks.

The squirrels, for their part, stop chasing each other and begin taunting the luckless dog.

I move off down the block.

The wind blows stronger, so there are bits of trash—old newspapers, coffee cups, McDonald's wrappers, and plastic bags—carried out into the street. One solitary black crow seems to be hanging, motionless, in midair above me, one leg tucked up to its belly, the claw curled like a tiny fist.

I struggle to get a cigarette lit. There's a bunch of giant blow-up Christmas decorations in the yard of a house built around a metal trailer. A generator groans ineffectually as the plastic Santa falls limp to one side and begins flapping like a flag in the wind. An equally unimpressive snow globe is bent in half, crushing the back hoof of one of the flattened reindeer.

The next house has a fake chimney propped atop its shingled roof with plastic Santa's legs sticking straight up, as though he were actively sliding headfirst into their fireplace. There's a sign, made up of colored lights just below it, wishing the entire neighborhood a "Merry Christmas."

The holidays are still over three weeks away, but nearly every house on the block is decorated.

At home we haven't gotten a tree yet, or put up any lights or anything. We've barely celebrated Christmas at all these last two years. Jane gets excited about it, naturally, and we pitch in to get her presents and watch Christmas movies and take her ice-skating at the Embarcadero.

But how could any of us ever be truly happy knowing that my brother is out there somewhere—terrified, alone?

That is why I'm here.

And I will not stop 'til I find him.

II.

DOTTY PETERSON'S HOUSE IS even smaller than ours—all dark paneling, with a wall of built-in bookshelves, stacked unevenly with paperback novels like you'd buy in a grocery store. There are also at least five or six cats roaming around the house. And way more cat furniture—those complicated, carpeted, always dirty-looking geometric structures—than people furniture. The cats are scraggly. They keep alternating between scratching themselves and pouncing on one another, fighting and squabbling.

The smell of cat piss burns like ammonia at the back of my throat.

But Dotty is very nice—just like she was on the phone. She makes me Lipton tea in a small porcelain cup—with cats printed on it, naturally. We sit together on a deeply sagging couch, the brown corduroy upholstery torn from countless cats' claws.

She's a large woman, with a sagging chin and neck hanging down. Her glasses are square and thick, so her narrow eyes are strangely magnified. She has short, dark, graying hair. Various cats jump on and off her lap as we talk.

"You poor dear," she says to me, alternately sipping her own cup of tea and eating from a tin of butter cookies on the coffee table. "I wish there was more I could do to help. I suppose you've talked to that Detective Marshall. He struck me as a capable man."

"No, not yet," I answer, though, of course, I recognize the name as the primary detective in charge of Teddy's case.

Dotty sits up straighter, smiling, as though she is actually quite excited by all this. It makes sense, I guess. She must be lonely here in this dark little house. I mean, maybe she has a husband or a girlfriend or something—but I kind of doubt it.

"Well, you should go talk to him. I imagine he'll tell you whatever you want to know. Why, I still have the business card he gave me on my refrigerator, I believe."

"From two years ago?"

"Certainly. It was such an excit—I mean, terrible tragedy. But I'm sure Detective Marshall will make time for you. It's just, they're so busy, you know, the police up in San Francisco. A case like your . . . your brother's, well, they usually accept whatever answer is the easiest. An open case looks bad for the department. I learned that watching *Law & Order*. It's so good. Have you seen it? I love that Jack McCoy."

She gestures toward the flat screen TV, which looks strangely out of place in this falling-apart living room that practically has mold growing out of the corners.

"No, I, uh, I haven't."

"Well, never mind. The point is, the police don't like having unsolved cases on their books. That's why they insist that Teddy . . . your brother . . . must have drowned. Even though I've told them over and over again what I saw. They refuse to believe it because . . . because they want everything neat and tidy, wrapped up with a little bow on it . . . You know what I mean?"

"So you don't think he drowned?"

Her hand reaches out and grabs mine suddenly. The feel of it is warm and sticky, so I want to pull away, but I don't want to be impolite.

"I *know* he didn't," she tells me, looking straight into my eyes. "And you're right to do this on your own."

I laugh awkwardly. "Really? I thought maybe I was being crazy."

"Not at all, not at all. The police can only do so much in these kinds of situations. They have limited time . . . and limited resources, too. You see, both my parents were killed by a hit-and-run driver when my sisters and I were little girls." She's still holding my hand and staring straight at me, and I see her eyes start to redden with tears. "The police did what they could, of course. But they never found the driver."

"Jesus," I say.

Her hand loosens its grip on mine, and she bows her head.

"Yes, well, we all have our crosses to bear. That's why, when I heard about what happened at the beach that day, I made up my mind to come forward and tell the police what I'd seen. In fact . . ."

She breaks off, glancing at me quickly, her whole face turning a deep purple color as she blushes all down her neck.

"I . . . I'm sorry . . ." She falters. "I didn't . . . I don't know how to say this to you, but . . . it's my fault. All of it. I knew it was going to happen."

Trembling, she takes up some tissues from a box on the end table and dabs at her eyes.

"What do you mean? You couldn't have known."

"Oh!" she says. "Oh, God, forgive me. I'm sorry. I'm so sorry."

She lurches across the empty space between us and, before I can react, I find myself with my head pressed firmly against her ample fucking bosom (covered, mercifully, by a gray sweatshirt with—of course—cats printed on it). She begins to cry then, holding me against her like that, and I wonder if maybe I'm not the only one who forgot to take their medication today.

"But you didn't know," I say, desperately trying to pull myself away. "You shouldn't blame yourself. I mean, if anyone's to blame, it's me, not you."

"Oh, that's sweet of you," she tells me, drying her eyes. "That's very kind of you. If you only knew how I've been torturing myself, day in and day out."

Yeah, me too, I think but don't say out loud.

"You see," she continues, "I hadn't meant to go to the beach at all. Only it was so hot, and you know I work as a tollbooth operator at the bridge? I decided to stop off on my way home. Of course, I'm not one for swimming, or sunbathing. But I like watching the ocean. I sat at one of the picnic tables—"

"Picnic tables?" My mind turns that around, trying to remember. "Where are there picnic tables?"

She smiles. "Why, just at the parking lot. I was sitting at the picnic tables, looking out at the ocean. I noticed the waves were getting bigger and bigger, and then a group of kids went running past me. They went up to play in the sand dunes, so when I saw your brother, at first I thought he must've come from that group of children."

"And you're sure?" I ask hurriedly. "You're sure it was Teddy?"

My words falter trying to pronounce his name. The backs of my eyes are burning now, imagining the beach, the waves, the sand dunes, the group of kids playing—and Teddy there with me, until I left him alone.

"I know it was him," she answers.

Her hand takes mine up again, and this time, I don't mind.

"The police showed me dozens of photos. I spoke with your

mom and dad. I remember them perfectly. They were such lovely people. And, yes, again, to answer your question, I am one hundred percent sure. It was him—red hair, freckles—about this tall . . ." She shows me with her free hand, holding at about her shoulder height from the ground.

"What was he doing?" I stammer.

"He was walking by himself. And then . . . and then a man came over and began talking to him. I couldn't hear what they were saying. The boy shook his head. I told the police that afterward. He shook his head . . . twice. And then the man took him by the arm and led him into that car."

"A white Ford Explorer," I say, the tears coming now so I can't fight them.

"That's right," she tells me, looking straight at me again. "That's right. And I knew. At the time, I knew. Something was not right. That's why I remembered it all as clearly as I did. Because I knew that something was wrong. And I did nothing. In my heart I felt it. I felt like I should stop that man from taking that child, but I didn't act. I failed. It is my fault."

She cries then, too, and we cry together.

"And the man?" I blurt out louder than I mean to, my voice cracking. "The man?"

Her head drops, and she clasps her hands together, releasing me.

"He was a tall man, balding on top, gray hair around the sides. He had a large nose and was wearing loose sweatpants and a sweatshirt. His face was hard, sunken in—no meat on his bones at all. But it was his eyes that stayed with me. His eyes were like . . ."

She stares off then, waving her arm absently in front of her, as though trying to catch the words out of the air.

"Like a black hole," she finally says. "Like emptiness."

I shiver, pulling my jacket tighter around me.

"Did . . . did he struggle?" I ask timidly.

She shakes her head again. "No. No. It wasn't like that. He just went with the man. They talked and then they got in the car together."

I nod.

She takes her cup up off the table and brings it to her mouth, but then replaces it without drinking.

"When you called me," she says, "I started thinking about what I should tell you. And I believe I received a sort of testimony, you understand? That I should share with you the answer—the real answer, to the only question there truly can be for anyone."

My breath catches. "Yes, no, I mean . . . You've already helped me so much. I don't know how to thank you."

I start trying to get myself up as if to go, but she just smiles, tapping my knee a few times, as though gently hammering me into the sofa.

"You don't need to thank me. Something brought us together today—something bigger than you or me."

"Uh-huh," I say dumbly.

"Do you know who can get you through this?" she asks, purring almost like one of her cats. "Do you know who you can rely on? Who your family can rely on? Who will save you? And who will save your brother?"

My head bobs up and down mechanically. I know what's coming, but there's nothing much I can do about it now.

"Jesus Christ," she says, not waiting for my answer. "Jesus Christ died on the cross to give us all everlasting life and take away our sins. Jesus is with *you,* always. He is with us all, always. We can either reject him, going it alone, or we can take him into our hearts and he will guide us to our rightful place in the Kingdom of Heaven."

I nod and smile, like a damn idiot, then get up from the couch. "Yes, well," I say, "thank you, but I really do have to get back. I'll let you know if I find anything."

She adjusts the glasses on her porcine nose and pushes herself up to standing. "But I'm not done. There's so much more I have to tell you."

She stares up at me, her eyes wet and red and pleading.

And then, suddenly, I can see—I can see why she was so eager to have me come down here today. I can see why she gave interviews to every paper and appeared on every news report about the kidnapping. I can see why she remembers it all as clearly as she does. I can see why she has Detective Marshall's business card on her refrigerator over two years later. And I can see why she continues to blame herself for not having stopped that man from taking Teddy.

She wants to be a part of the story.

It's as simple as that.

She lives alone here. She works collecting tolls at the bridge. She has her cats, her church, her TV shows.

Witnessing Teddy's kidnapping must've made her feel, maybe for the first time ever, truly important.

So of course she would think that God had some greater purpose in letting my brother get taken like that. Because, for her, the greater purpose was that she, finally, got to be somebody.

They put her picture in the paper.

She got to be on TV—not just once, but many times.

"I have to go," I say. "I'm sorry."

I start toward the door.

"No, wait—"

Her hand reaches out, as if to stop me.

But I don't stop.

I keep on going.

I open the door.

And I don't turn back.

12.

BY THE TIME I GET home, my mom and dad are out at a movie with Janey, so I'm left on my own for dinner. But in all my nervousness and whatever, I find that I'm really not hungry.

I'm going crazy sitting here by myself. So I finally decide, like, fuck it, I might as well go to Preston's party.

I clean myself up as much as possible and put on what I would consider my coolest clothes—just a pair of jeans and a ripped-up T-shirt over a thermal undershirt—and a big fur-lined army jacket, because it's freezing outside.

Of course, I know it's fucking stupid to be going to this thing, but I go on anyway—walking down the avenues for a couple of blocks, crossing over Lake Street and heading up into Sea Cliff where every house is the size of a fucking castle and no lights are ever on in any of the windows and no music is ever heard on the street. People here are so rich, they're able to shut the world out completely and to shut themselves out from the world.

In our neighborhood, at least, people yell and laugh and fight and burn things and have dead chickens hanging in their storefront windows.

Here it's all imitation Italian villas and imitation French chateaus and imitation Bavarian estates and imitation Spanish whatever-you-call-them and imitation Japanese-style houses like Eliza used to live in. It's funny how rich people like to pretend so much. Rich people are like little kids—like Teddy used to be, with his toy cars and action figures and the Superman cape he made out of a bathroom towel. With enough money, they can be anything they want to be.

I remember Eliza's dad wanted to be a kind of samurai sushi chef—which is why they had that house like some Shinto temple.

Preston's parents want to be crazy bohemians traveling all over the world. And they can do it, too, 'cause they have the money. They can be whatever they want to be.

While the rest of us are stuck being what we are.

I begin to see cars parked up and down the street—cars that must belong to people attending Preston's party—lining the golf course and filling the upper parking lot of the Palace of the Legion of Honor.

Preston's always been super popular, and even though I know for sure none of these people are anywhere near as close to him as I am, I can't help but feel a little jealous—or just annoyed maybe. Because it's not like any of these kids actually give a shit about him. Not really. All they care about is the fact that he has a nice house and his parents are never around.

The house *is* nice, though, it's true: built alone on the jagged cliffs, surrounded by cypress trees and low-hanging fog, with a Gothic-style pitched roof and marble columns and all sorts of stained-glass windows and skylights.

I go in through the front gate, and there are some upperclassmen hanging out around the fountain, smoking a blunt, I think, and I wave to them meekly. They don't wave back or acknowledge me, and I think maybe I should turn around. I mean, really I hate parties and I'm not sure what the hell I'm even doing here.

It's strange to be with kids my age, trying so hard to be cool and fucking popular—especially when I just came from meeting with that woman who actually witnessed my brother being kidnapped.

The way she described that man. It's so terrible to think about. And yet she still tried to tell me that there is some kind of God looking out for us—protecting us, even.

Can that really be the way it works? I mean, I'm not saying I don't believe in God—I really do like the idea of some higher power like that. But I don't think it has anything to do with my brother being taken by some psycho—or these jackasses standing around smoking weed.

Looking at these kids standing in their designer fucking clothes, smoking their designer fucking pot, I can't help feeling like I want to tear the whole world apart.

It was a mistake to come; I can see that immediately.

I should leave.

Only . . .

Preston did say that Eliza was going to be here.

Not that it matters.

What matters is finding Teddy.

What matters is bringing my family back together.

Eliza doesn't matter at all.

But my heart beats painfully fast just thinking about her.

The idea of seeing her again is . . . almost more than I can stand.

My hands shake as I hold them out in front of me.

Past those boys smoking the blunt, past the fountain, and the statues, and the marble staircase, and the front door, Eliza is there—or, at least, she's supposed to be.

And Preston says she wants to see me, to talk to me, to apologize.

Over two years have gone by, and so much has changed.

I ring the buzzer.

13.

INSIDE, THE MUSIC IS loud, so Preston has to shout, "Yo, Miles, what's up?"

He has on this crazy knit hat that's, like, all these different colors of yarn stitched together.

"Come on in, man," he says.

We walk in through the front entrance and up the stairs past the rows of framed photographs of Preston and his mom and dad. Tonight, since they're not home, we have free range of the entire house. We keep on walking up to the main dining room and kitchen, where I see maybe a hundred kids hanging out.

"Damn, there are so many people here," I tell him, dragging hard on my cigarette.

He laughs. "Hell yeah, there are. I told everyone to invite

as many friends as they wanted. This is gonna be the party of the century."

He leads me through the throngs of people dancing and whatever while the rapper dude on the stereo is singing, *"Shake ya ass! Watch ya self! Shake ya ass! Show me what you workin' with!"*

"Is this really happening right now?" I whisper to him, but I know the answer and, anyway, he doesn't hear me.

On the little center island in the kitchen are a bunch of bottles of different hard liquors and orange juice and stuff, and the music is so loud, and there are all these bodies moving against mine. I suddenly feel that pain coming back in my stomach, and then I remember I didn't eat anything before taking my goddamn medication and so that must be why I'm getting so sick like this. Usually I'd try to space it out, but tonight, since I knew I was leaving, I took them all at the same time—the four tablets of lithium, the three capsules of Prozac, the two Lamictal, the two Zyprexa, the two Depakote, and the one Abilify. And so they are burning like an oil fire through the lining of my intestines.

"Hey!" I yell. "Hey, do you have anything to eat here, man? I'm sorry."

Preston hands me a drink in a red plastic cup saying, "Here, shoot this, dude, you'll feel better."

I repeat my question, but he just keeps saying, "Shoot it!"

And so I fucking do, and it burns going down and I cough

and I feel it like more fire in my belly. I imagine it mixing together with all the undigested medication, forming this acid substance that eats through the lining of my stomach and then comes spilling out through my skin right there onto the dark-colored tile.

"Man, I'm serious, do you have any food here I could eat?"

Preston takes his shot and shakes his head and says real loud, "BLAH! Yeah, sure, I think. Look in the fridge, man, you can have whatever."

"Cool, thanks."

I start walking over, but it's like that shot was injected straight into my bloodstream, 'cause I feel dizzy and weak. I crush out my cigarette on the floor 'cause I can't stand the smell of it for one more second.

Preston has gone now, and I'm all alone with these people moving together like some giant, pulsing organic life-form crawling out of the primordial sea, taking its first steps on land, writhing and gyrating and secreting fluids.

The electric lights seem to pulse and crackle with the sound of the bass thumping on the stereo. I close my eyes and reach out my hand and fall onto the tile. I wretch some, but nothing comes out, thank God, because then there's a voice and it's calling out to me, "Miles . . . Miles . . . Are you okay?"

I open my eyes.

I'm not sure if this is another hallucination or what, but she is there, crouching over me.

"Miles . . . What's wrong?"

She puts her hand on my forehead, and it feels so cool and calming somehow. I smell that old familiar smell of her—like shampoo and clean laundry and I'm not sure what else.

"Eliza?" I say. "Is that you?"

She smiles brightly.

"Yeah, of course."

She helps me to my feet.

"Come on," she says, her voice calming. "You wanna go get some air?"

I nod.

And we walk together back outside.

14.

THE WIND IS BLOWING strong across the stone court-yard and Eliza is shivering, so I give her my jacket.

"You sure?" she asks, pulling it tighter around her shoulders.

"Yeah, I'm sorry, I just didn't eat enough. We can go back inside."

She shakes her head. "No, not yet. I wanna talk to you," she says.

Her voice has gotten deeper somehow. Her black hair is pushed back behind her ears.

I struggle for breath a little, but I'm trying to hold it to-gether, so I light another cigarette, looking down into those shining green-blue eyes of hers.

"Hey, I'm taller than you," I say, smiling.

"Yeah, I wonder when that happened?"

She takes a step closer to me and turns and I can see her

profile—her nose so delicate and sculptural, her full lips. I think for the billionth time how goddamn beautiful she is.

"Can I, uh . . . can I have one of those?" she asks, looking back at me.

"Y-yeah, sure."

I hand her a cigarette and then try to light it for her, but the wind's too strong so she has to do it herself.

Somehow that feels like a really big failure on my part.

"I've missed you, Miles," she says, handing back the lighter, and our eyes meet and then dart away quickly.

"Me too."

She sits down on the step and zips up my big army coat. "I've been wanting to see you."

I sit next to her and I can feel the heat from her body.

"M-me too."

I keep repeating it like a goddamn idiot.

Me too. Me too. Me too.

"Have you really?" she asks, leaning against me.

"Yeah, totally."

But there's an overpowering smell, like rotting flesh, and something burning that seems to come up from the ground around me, inexplicably, and I reel back.

"I heard about what happened to you," she says plainly.

I move away from her, but not because of what she said; it's just that the smell is almost gagging me. But she takes it the wrong way.

"Oh, I'm sorry," she says. "We don't have to talk about that."

"No, no, it's okay. Sorry. It's just my stomach."

She nods. "Are you on a lot of medication?"

I try holding myself very still again the nausea.

"Uh, yeah, I guess."

She smiles sweetly. "Well, I understand. I know it's not the same thing, but I've been seeing a therapist, too, for a couple months now. And she wants me to go see, like, one of those psychopharma . . . whatever they're called?"

"Psychopharmacologists."

"Exactly."

I drag on my cigarette, exhaling through my nose.

"What are you seeing 'em for?" I ask. "Are you depressed?" And then I add, quickly, "That is, if you don't mind my asking."

She leans against me again, and I watch her fingers twitching as she ashes her cigarette over and over.

"No, I don't mind. It's nice to be able to finally talk about it with someone. None of my friends understand."

"Yeah, none of mine do, either."

"*Right?* I missed you, Miles. Remember how much we used to talk on the phone and stuff?"

"Of course. Every night."

My head is kind of spinning, so I rub my temple with the side of my thumb like I'm trying to put the world on pause.

"So what happened?" I ask hesitantly, not wanting to upset her too much by pushing the subject.

She breathes and smokes and breathes some more. Then she finally says, "You have to promise not to tell anyone else, okay?"

I give her my promise. "Believe me, I don't talk to anyone anyway."

She laughs a little. "Well . . . the thing is, my dad left."

A cold sweat has broken out all up and down my body now because of the goddamn medication.

"He met someone else," she says.

"Jesus."

"I know, right? The fucker. After all those years of fooling around and lying and everything, he finally just told my mom straight out he didn't love her anymore."

"Jesus."

My new fucking mantra.

"He moved out that same night, and we were, like, stuck, just the two of us, in this big town house off the French Quarter. My mom barely left her room for three months."

"Jesus."

"Yeah. She was . . . Well, I mean, seriously, don't tell anyone this, but she was even hospitalized. It was the doctors who thought we should move back here. At least in the city she has some family, you know? You remember my aunt who lives in Marin?"

"Of course."

Eliza's aunt is this cool old lesbian who works as a park ranger out at the Point Reyes National Seashore. Eliza's family took me on a few weekend trips up there when we were kids.

I lean back against the iron railing. "So who was she? Another bimbo waitress?"

Eliza laughs. "No. She's actually a chef, too, if you can believe that."

"I'd have thought with your dad's ego being like it is, that would be way too threatening."

She smiles. "You remember that, too, huh?"

"I remember everything."

She stops smiling.

"I know," she says finally. "Miles, I'm sorry."

And I say, "No, that's not what I meant. But . . . anyway . . . I'm sorry, too."

She's closer to me now, so I can hear the shallow sound of her breathing against the cold night air. I remember when we went to Hawaii together, back when we were kids. Her mom paid for this cool Hawaiian guy to take us horseback riding along the tops of these cliffs overlooking the ocean. But at one point, when our guide was busy closing the gate behind us, Eliza's horse took off running and then, not even knowing what I was doing, I kicked my horse hard with my heels and went galloping after her. It was my first time ever being on horseback, but I had to catch her. So I got my horse right up beside hers and somehow that made the horse she was on slow down and relax, until finally we were both able to stop.

She was breathing fast then. I remember it—like she was hyperventilating, so bad she could barely even speak. "Take a deep breath," I told her. "Come on, you can do it, just take a deep breath."

And she did. She did what I told her. She breathed deep and long and slow.

I listen to her breathing now—slower, easier.

I kick the toe of my boot into the ground, trying to think up something to say to change the subject.

"Uh . . . did your, uh . . . dad stay in New Orleans?"

"Yeah, and you know how my dad used to be so obsessed with Japan? Now it's like he's totally changed and suddenly he doesn't care at all about the Japanese stuff and he's become totally obsessed with New Orleans. I swear, he's gonna start talking with an accent before long."

We both laugh at that.

"You know . . . I . . . uh . . . Your dad . . . I mean . . . he was always pretty distant. And he was terrible to your mom . . . and to you . . . really. So maybe you guys are better off this way?"

"That's exactly what I told my mom," she says. "I knew you'd understand."

She takes my hand in hers for a second, and the feel of her is warm and electric all over my body.

"Well," I tell her, "I am sorry this is happening to you. I know it must be hard."

"Yeah, thanks." She tilts her head to one side. "Anyway," she adds, "at least we got to move back here, right?"

I nod, thinking that maybe I really should make getting food a priority—because the nausea is not letting up. The pain is still in my stomach, and now the veins in my skull feel all swelled with blood, squeezing in at my temples so goddamn tight. With each beat of my heart, it's like the veins clamp down even harder and I see this bright light flashing in the darkness when I close my eyes.

"Hey, are you all right?" she asks me.

"Yeah . . . no," I say, standing up as slowly as I can so I don't do anything embarrassing, like maybe pass out completely. "I'm fine. You wanna . . . you wanna go get something to eat?"

"Sure," she says, smiling.

"I can make something inside," I tell her, not wanting to make her leave if she doesn't want to. "Or we could go to Video Café. They're open twenty-four hours."

She nods. "Okay, yes, let's do that."

Her body brushes against mine as she starts to walk, and I feel this warmth in me just from the slightest touch. That strange rotting smell has gone, and I think maybe this might actually work out. After all, she seems the same. I mean, different—but the same. The same Eliza. And I think maybe I'm not that different, either.

It's just like it used to be.

But then Preston's front door opens and a bunch of kids holding forties come pouring out into the courtyard with us. They're seniors I know only by sight, but tonight, because of Eliza being so goddamn beautiful, they seem eager to talk. In fact, one of them even knows my name.

"Yo, what's up, Miles? Who's this you got here?"

He's sloppy drunk, but still handsome, I think. At least, I imagine Eliza must think he's handsome. He has his hair all shaved around the sides and long in front, sticking up straight, kind of like a pompadour. His teeth are bright white in the darkness, and he smiles big and reaches out a hand to shake Eliza's.

"Hey, I'm Kevin," he says.

She shakes his hand, and then the other guys all introduce themselves, too—to her, not to me.

Besides Kevin, I don't process any of their names enough to remember what they are.

But then the one dude with the stupid hipster straw hat pulls out a blunt from behind his ear and asks us if we want any.

Eliza presses in closer to me and kind of looks up for approval, as if somehow it's up to me—I guess 'cause I was the one who wanted to leave so bad.

"Yeah, go ahead," I say, and she smiles and leans against me, and the guy fires the blunt up and it's like someone is driving nails into either side of my brain, and so I press the palm of my hand against my forehead.

Eliza hits the blunt and then she coughs real cute-sounding and all the guys laugh.

She hits it again before passing it off and then standing up on her tiptoes and whispering in my ear, "Hey, you wanna go to that restaurant now?"

The two of us walk out through the iron gate and down the street past the wall of boxwood hedges surrounding the golf course.

Beyond the protection of the courtyard, the wind is blowing even stronger, and I shiver.

"Here," she says, handing my coat back to me.

I want to take it, but I feel like maybe she'll think I'm lame or something if I do.

"No, it's okay," I say. "You keep it." But the cold is all the way inside me now, and that headache has gotten so bad that it's like whatever had been pounding there before has now just clamped down, so I have to keep my eyes pretty near shut.

I throw my cigarette out, but that doesn't help, either, and as much as I want to be hanging out with her, I'm suddenly wondering if maybe I should just go home and lie down.

So I stop and I breathe and I grit my teeth together, putting my hands on my knees and saying, "Hey, Eliza, look, I'm sorry. I want to hang out with you and get dinner and everything. I really do and . . . and it's so great seeing you, but I have this terrible headache right now for some reason. I think maybe it's all the medicine . . ."

I force my eyes open enough to see her smile, and her teeth are white and straight and perfect.

"Yeah, you look a little sick."

I breathe, straining. "I'm so sorry, 'Liza."

She nods. "No, I understand. I'll let you go. It's just so great to see you again. And, look . . . uh . . . Miles, I know I was terrible to you when we were younger. Really, I'm not sure why you put up with me like you did, but I am so, so sorry."

"Please, no," I say, but hoarsely, so I have to clear my throat before continuing. "You don't need to apologize. I understand. Anyway, I wasn't putting up with you. I loved—I mean, I . . . I liked hanging out with you."

She touches me, just for a moment, and I feel it coursing through me again.

The sound of the wind is like the ocean waves breaking through the treetops.

The fog light at the mouth of the bay flashes across the dark silhouette of Eliza's body pressed close to mine.

"I think I was just too afraid then," she tells me, looking straight ahead.

I laugh through my nose. "Afraid of me?"

"Yeah, totally. You always seemed so perfect or something. Like you had this perfect family and you were so . . . good . . . so sweet . . . so *perfect*."

I stare down, suddenly, at the hole widening on the side of my boot where I can see black sock starting to stick out.

"Yeah, well, not anymore. Now I'm just crazy."

She looks up and her eyes close and open, and she whispers, "I like you, so much, Miles. I've always liked you."

She lifts up on the balls of her feet and suddenly she's pressing her full lips into mine and she's kissing me.

It's happening so fast, and I want to be able to just hold on to every fucking second. I mean, I've been waiting for this kiss with Eliza for my whole life, but now that it's actually happening, it's like I feel strangled somehow. We slide our tongues in and out, but the lack of oxygen to my brain is making the veins swell and pound and fucking press down even more. I feel dizzy, and something gags me at the back of my throat and I have to push her away.

I drop to my knees, hitting the pavement hard as vomit comes charging up out of my throat.

"Oh, my God! What's happening?" she yells.

I throw up over and over and over, retching, spitting up chunks of stringy I don't even know what—like pieces of shredded kelp and seaweed, all green and reddish purple.

Gawwghh is the noise I make. And then, "I'm sorry. I'm so sorry."

And then the vomit comes again.

I lie with my face on the cold, rough concrete.

I spit and punch the ground with my fist.

"Just go away," I finally say. "I'm sorry. Please."

Her voice comes out pretty hysterical-sounding. "No. I'm not leaving you."

But there's barf everywhere, and I'm so sick and disgusted with myself, I yell at her, "I want you to leave, all right? Just go away."

She takes a step back.

"GO!" I yell.

I hear what sounds like her bursting into tears.

And then her boots running away from me down the street.

15.

SOMEONE CALLS OUT FROM behind me and I turn, angry at first, just wanting to be left alone.

"I'm all right," I groan, struggling to get to my feet.

"Jesus Christ," the voice says. "What happened?"

I turn to see Jackie, wearing a wool hat, gloves, and a big knit sweater, walking quickly toward me.

"Nothing," I tell her. "I'm all right."

She smiles and shivers and crosses her arms and says, "Brrr, it's so fucking cold out here. Come back inside. We can hide out in Preston's room."

The streetlamp overhead switches on so that Jackie is silhouetted by the soft glow and the fog coming down. She reaches out to take my hand and I do not pull away. Not from her.

"I'm sick," I mumble. "I just got sick."

"Yeah, no shit. Come on. We'll clean you up."

I fumble to get a cigarette lit, and Jackie takes one from my pack.

"I gotta go home."

"Well, then let me drive you."

"You sure?"

"Yeah, of course."

"What are you doing out here?" I ask. "Did you see Eliza?"

She speaks softly, like you would to a child—which, I guess, is kind of what I am. "Yeah. I ran into her coming in. She told me you were sick."

"Great."

"Anyway, I needed an excuse to get out of there."

"You mean the party?"

"Yeah, yeah . . . the party. And, I don't know . . . Preston, too."

We cross over in front of the golf course and walk down onto the carefully manicured lawn toward her little Volkswagen.

While I may have barfed on the girl of my dreams and totally humiliated myself, I think, at least I have Jackie.

And she has me.

I walk quickly around to the passenger side of her car. There is vomit still wet on my shirtfront. And I still want to fucking cry.

16.

MY MOM IS AWAKE when I get home—sitting in the dark, drinking white wine, and watching *Double Indemnity* on TV for, like, the billionth time. She seems a little drunk, honestly, as I stumble in, and I guess that's probably why she doesn't freak out at the sight of me as much as she normally would. Because me coming home covered in puke like this would be just the type of thing to send her into a panic. Seriously, my mom is absolutely the worst person to be with in any kind of crisis situation. She completely loses her shit—going from zero to full-blown hysteria in, like, half a second.

But tonight, surprisingly, she remains relatively calm.

She pauses the movie and stands up, coming around to put her cool hand on my hot forehead.

"I think you have a fever. Are you okay? What happened?"

The smell of her is so familiar and comforting that I choke up. "I got sick," I say, and then I burst into tears.

"Oh, sweetie. Come here, love," she says, putting her arms around me.

"But I'm all gross."

She tells me not to worry, and so I cry into her sweatshirt and the warmth of her as she holds me and I feel so tired—so completely exhausted.

"What happened?" she asks. "Were you drinking?"

I sniffle. "No, it's my medicine. I forgot to eat before going to the party and I took all my meds at once and . . . I got sick."

"Hey," she says, kissing the top of my head and shushing me gently. "It happens to everyone, all right? Don't be so hard on yourself."

Oh, yeah, I think, *tons of people decide to take their psych meds all at once and then blow their only chance to be with the girl they've loved basically forever by puking on her.*

Happens all the time.

I feel like digging a hole in the backyard and then curling up in there and just wasting away until there is nothing left.

"Here," she whispers. "You go get cleaned up, and I'll make you something to eat, all right?"

"No. Don't worry about it."

"You need to eat," she says. "It's no problem." And then, "Only, uh . . . try to be quiet going in your room. Jane wanted to sleep in there 'cause she was having a bad dream. Is that okay?"

I nod.

It makes sense; she'd been sharing her room with Teddy since she was three years old. No wonder she can't sleep in there.

I go into my room and manage to get out some pajamas from the drawer without waking Janey up. The sound of her breathing is soft and calming in the darkness.

By the time I take a quick shower and brush my teeth and put on my pajamas, my mom's already finished making me a grilled cheese sandwich and some hot chocolate. I thank her, and then we sit down together on the couch. My mom turns the movie back on, and I eat silently and lean against her.

I watch Fred MacMurray climbing the steps to Barbara Stanwyck's Spanish-style house somewhere in 1940s Los Angeles. When he rings the doorbell, I know that she will answer. And I know that by the end of the film she will have killed him.

I settle in to watch the movie, trying not to think of anything else. Fred MacMurray is being suckered into committing a murder for this woman he barely even knows—but has fallen hopelessly in love with. For him, the money is secondary. All he cares about is her—and all she cares about is herself. It's an old story. Adam conned by Eve into eating the apple.

The images flash black and white across the screen.

My mom whispers, "I love you, sweetie."

I close my eyes and open them. "I love you, too, Mom."

We watch the movie together.

And for now, at least, that is enough.

17.

THE SOUND OF JANEY screaming wakes me up early, before it's all the way light outside. She's sleeping in my bed, and I'm on a blow-up mattress, so I get up onto my knees and put a hand on her sweating forehead.

She jerks and twitches in her sleep, yelling, "STOP! STOP!"

"Jane," I say. "It's just a dream."

Her eyes open slowly.

"Miles," she says, wrapping her small arms around my neck and crying out. "It was awful."

She hugs me, and I inhale the smell of her, which is like peppermint and fresh-cut grass.

"You had a bad dream?"

Her head nods up and down as she pokes her bottom lip out and sniffles. "Sharks."

A shiver runs through me, thinking about the ocean that day—about Teddy.

"I'm afraid of sharks, too," I say.

She smiles.

Posters of different jazz musicians are hung up against the patterned wallpaper that looks like some kind of tree with branches like lungs and leaves like a hundred eyes wide-open. There's a mirror on one wall that reflects the wallpaper pattern on the other so it looks like a framed painting. I also have a collection of taxidermy insects behind glass cases. Beetles, mostly, and butterflies—and a bat framed with its wings spread out hanging next to the open closet with no door. There's a replica of a human skull on my dresser next to a set of blown-glass medicine bottles from the twenties or thirties.

"Hey," I say, standing all the way up and stretching. "You wanna go out for coffee and donuts? Or, uh, hot chocolate and donuts? I have a little bit of money left from my last paycheck."

She smiles and nods excitedly. Her eyes get brighter.

"All right, well," I continue, "go get dressed warm and we'll go. But be quiet, okay? So you don't wake up Mom and Dad."

She pushes the covers back. "No way. I won't wake 'em up."

She hops out of bed, wearing a flannel nightgown our grandmother sewed for her, and tiptoes over to the next room while I throw on clothes and an army-navy surplus dark blue peacoat. I peer out the blinds and see the tall grass and overgrown weeds are wet and heavy with dew. The sun has yet to rise over the curve of the world to the east, but its rays fill the morning sky with white light turning gray around the edges as it fights to overtake the darkness of night.

It will be a clear day. I can see that already.

There are no clouds. No fog. The sun filling the white-gray sky with the beginnings of color.

I feel an odd sense of hope.

But then I see the crows, gathering on the telephone wires—waiting, watching me through the window.

Their black eyes dart in every direction. They scratch and claw. They call out. They cover the wires, just as the wires cover the skyline.

Janey tugs on the sleeve of my coat, startling me a little. "Wow, look at all those crows."

I close the blinds, take a step back from the window. "What? What did you say?"

She smiles sweetly. "The crows. Those are crows, right? Or are they ravens?"

I crouch down closer to her. "You can see them, too?"

She laughs. "Of course, silly."

I stand up straight, feeling relieved.

I take her hand and lead her out into the still, early morning. We cross the street and the sun is bright and I think that here, with my sister, everything is okay.

18.

WORK DRAGS ON FOR fucking ever.

The manager has me working in the back room, unloading canned goods—checking their different prices and sticking stickers on them with a pricing gun and marking off the quantities on the invoice sheet. It's dark, and I squint my eyes and wish I were home and keep checking my phone to see what time it is, even though that just makes my shift seem to go all the more slowly. Not to mention that a boring-ass task like this gives me that much more time to replay last night's events over in my mind—an endless loop of me saying stupid shit to Eliza and then barfing on her, again and again, over and over.

So I go on unpacking the boxes and pointlessly trying to block the memory out—until I finally check my phone again and I see that I have a text message I somehow missed.

From fucking Ordell.

He writes in all capital letters: *DUDE, DID YOU PUKE ON ELIZA LINDBERG? LOL. CALL ME!!!*

I read it again.

I wonder if maybe my mind is playing a trick on me—if this is just some kind of paranoid delusion like the goddamn crows.

But then, as if on cue, the phone chimes right there in my hand.

Another text.

I'm serious, dude. Call me. Everyone's talking about it!!!

Again with the three exclamation marks.

My heart pounds loudly in my ears so that everything else is blotted out around me. A cold sweat breaks out at the back of my neck.

I strip off my apron and the sweater I'm wearing and my thermal undershirt. But still I'm flushed and sweating, and so I leave the boxes there and I go out the back door, not even caring if my manager comes and yells at me.

The day is clear and the wind is strong and the light feels distant and cold and pale. The smell of the garbage from the large metal Dumpster in the alley is sickening, so I walk around to the residential street behind the market, sitting on the curb and breathing heavily, rocking my body back and forth. I rock there and feel the cold and try to figure out what the hell I'm going to do.

Could Eliza really have told everyone what happened?

I mean, it's not that I care what other people think, particularly; it's just disappointing that she wouldn't want to—I don't know—protect me?

I light a cigarette then and the smoke fills my lungs and my fingers twitch and shake.

The crows are in the branches of the bare, skinny trees planted in square patches of dirt in the sidewalk. The wires crisscross and crackle across the white stucco apartment complexes.

My eyes close and open. I try to make the images disappear, but it's never any fucking good. My mind unravels like a ball of string rolling down an unending staircase.

There's a dead squirrel lying torn apart in the middle of the street, and the crows pick through the still-bloody carcass, fighting loudly over the very best pieces.

I turn away and smoke and try to focus on the cold and the wind and the gritty asphalt beneath my boots. The curb where I'm sitting has been painted a dark green, but the color is faded and completely washed away in places.

A car drives past out front, and I turn to see the crows quickly scatter—only to reconvene over the mess of dead squirrel a few seconds later.

I stand up then and stamp my foot.

"GET OUT OF HERE!" I yell, feeling this surge of heat and anger from out of nowhere. "GO ON! GET OUT!"

Before I can even think about what I'm doing, I run out and yell louder, and the crows squawk at me and fly off.

I stand over the squirrel's lifeless body and clench my fists as though just daring the crows to try to take another shot at it.

But they don't.

My phone vibrates in my pocket, and I look to see that Preston's calling.

I decide I can't fucking deal with it, though, so I don't answer. A few seconds later, the phone chimes again. A text message. From Preston.

Hey, man. You all right? I gave your number to Eliza. I hope you don't mind. Are you sick???

I laugh at that.

Three question marks.

I don't write him back.

I finish my cigarette and go back inside.

The boxes are waiting.

None of this matters compared to Teddy, of course.

I know that.

I do.

But it hurts fucking bad.

And so I try to figure out what the hell I'm gonna do.

19.

BY THE TIME I get home the sun has nearly set on the horizon, so the brightest stars are already shining through the settling dark and the faint orange glow of city lights.

Because Janey and I can't start watching the movies I rented (*Harold and Maude* and *Being There,* my favorite Hal Ashby films) until after dinner, we are busy working together on a drawing on a card table set up next to the fireplace. The drawing we're doing is part of a larger project. I mean, it's kind of silly, really, but we're trying to put a comic book together. It's the story of these two characters she created—they're 1920s flapper girls named Mabel and Pearl. Honestly, Janey draws way better than I do. But I try to keep up.

My mom has taken a pill and gone to bed, apparently, and so I put on that Washington Phillips record that I bought the other day at Amoeba. I'm not sure what my mom was talking about. The music's not depressing at all. If anything, this guy must've been, like, a preacher or something, because every song is about God and Jesus and how great everything is going to be in heaven. I'd love to be able to believe in something like that. Plus, the man's voice is so sweet and pure and beautiful.

It's a good album.

"Hey, if you like this, you should check out these other records, too."

My dad walks over and crouches down next to the dark wood cabinet where he keeps his vinyl collection.

"Here," he says, piling a couple albums up on the table next to our drawing.

My dad is wearing a collared dress shirt rolled up to the elbows and open at the neck, flannel pajama bottoms, and plush, furry slippers. The pajamas are loose and hanging off him a little.

"Blind Willie Johnson," he says, standing up straighter to show me one of the records. "He really was blind."

Janey's gap-tooth smile is just the greatest, and my dad musses her hair with his large, calloused hands.

"And check this out," he says, passing her one final record. "Robert Johnson. People say he made a deal with the devil. That's how he learned to play the blues."

"Wow," Jane says. "Can we listen to this now?"

"Sure."

"Here, I got it," I tell my dad. I take the record from him and carry it over to where the turntable is set up.

"You guys hungry?" he asks.

"Yeah," says Janey.

"Yeah, me too, I guess," I say.

He goes to open the refrigerator and kind of grumbles, "Hmmm, slim pickings in here. How about some fried egg sandwiches? And bacon?"

I put the record on, and it crackles and pops loudly as the guitar music starts to play. The singing is pained and full of gravel and broken glass and dust and mud. It is beautiful.

Jane keeps on drawing while I go over to the kitchen to help my dad fry up the bacon. He makes some black coffee on the electric burner and some hot chocolate for Janey, then he cooks up a bunch of thick pieces of wheat bread in the grease from the bacon and fries the eggs right there in the same pan. Really, there's not that much I can do to help but just make the plates up.

"Hey," my dad says to me. "If you want, maybe you and me can play some music together later. Pull out the ol' guitars."

I smile. "That'd be great."

He lays the bacon and egg sandwiches out on the plates, and I pour the coffee and cocoa and then go over to turn on the TV.

Janey sits next to me on the couch, and my dad sits on the floor. He always likes to watch *60 Minutes* on Sunday nights, so we all watch it together. There's that part at the beginning where the anchors take turns saying, "I'm Steve Kroft," and, "I'm Lesley Stahl." And Teddy would always jump in, saying, "And I'm Teddy Cole." He thought that was just the funniest thing ever.

But now it's like we all have to talk over the opening so there isn't time to think about it.

"Thanks, Dad," Jane says. "This sandwich is really good."

"Miles helped, too," he answers, and she says, "Thank you, Miles."

And I tell her she's welcome.

We all watch the show and eat together and the fire is going and the wind rattles the screen door outside.

Everything is so nice like this, right now, with my family, and I wish I could just stay in this moment forever and never have to deal with Eliza or medication or doctors or go back to school, and never have to do anything ever again except to be here with my dad and sister . . .

And Teddy, of course . . . Teddy would be here.

He would be watching the show with us like he used to.

And then my mom would be here, too, just like she used to.

Someday it will be like that again.

Someday soon.

So I kiss Jane's forehead quickly and take her and my dad's plates and go wash them in the hot water in the sink. My phone is there on the counter, and I see the little blue missed-call light is blinking. I dry my hands on a checkered dishcloth and pick up my phone—even though I know I probably shouldn't, that I should just forget everything until tomorrow.

But I can't.

I can't do that.

The number is one I don't recognize, but it's got a 415 area code, which is San Francisco. I scroll through the menu options and then dial my voice mail, waiting, my stomach tight, my lungs contracted.

Her voice sounds sweet and beautiful and sexy even through the slight electronic distortion of my phone.

It's Eliza, of course.

She says that right off: *"Miles, hey, it's Eliza. Call me back, okay? I'm so sorry people are talking about this. Please know I didn't mean to tell anyone. I was just worried about you last night. But I should've just kept my mouth shut. Can you forgive me? And . . . uh . . . please. I want to hang out with you again. And I don't want you to be, you know, embarrassed at all, all right? You didn't do anything wrong. Do you want to, like, get coffee after school tomorrow maybe? Okay, thanks, Miles. It was so good to see you again. And . . . I don't know. Shoot . . . just, uh, call me. Okay? Bye."*

I erase the message quickly.

My hands tremble.

"You all right, Mie?" my dad calls from the living room.

"Y-yeah . . . I'm fine. I'll be right there."

"What are you doing?" Janey asks.

"Uh, nothing . . . I gotta take my medicine. It's okay. Just keep watching. I'll be back."

I leave my phone on the counter and walk into the bathroom and turn the lights on. The bulb overhead is out, but the one above the small mirror flickers on after a moment. There're some tiles with painted pink roses and white daisies all lined up at about eye level. The sink is stained and the faucet is white with calcium deposits. I open the top drawer and take out the different prescription bottles. Fluoxetine, 60 mg per day, which is just generic Prozac, an antidepressant, and then there's the Lamictal, 200 mg a day, which is a mood stabilizer. Then there's the lithium, 800 mg a day, and the Depakote, 300 mg a day, which build something called gray matter, whatever that is, and are supposed to help with the racing, paranoid, delusional thinking. And then there's the Abilify, 10 mg a day, which is specifically for schizophrenia. And the Zyprexa, 10 mg a day, the newest of the drugs. It's supposed to make you put on a ton of weight once you start taking it, but it hasn't for me at all. I'm just skin and bones.

The mirror reflects my sunken image, my eyes swollen and bloodshot. The color around my pupils is a golden yellowish brown. I stare straight into my own eyes. I turn on the tap so the cold water can run a minute. There's an empty plastic cup next to the toothbrushes, and I fill it with water. The light flickers overhead.

When I close my eyes there's an image projected on the back of my eyelids of Eliza the way she looked yesterday. I see her smiling. I see her leaning forward to kiss me. I see her and I reach out and take her hand in mine. There is the smell of her there with me suddenly. I inhale deeply and take the smell of her into my mouth and down the back of my throat and into my lungs and into my belly.

I remember that smell so clearly from when we were kids together. When her mom and dad were driving us back from the beach one time, I remember Eliza falling asleep with her head on my shoulder and her hair getting all tangled in my mouth and I wanted her to stay sleeping like that forever on me.

But last night should have been even better.

Last night she actually kissed me.

It really did happen.

I open my eyes.

I can still feel her with me.

And I want to keep feeling her with me.

I want that more than anything.

Maybe someday, after I find Teddy and he's safely home, then I can start worrying about girls and all that normal high school stuff.

For now, I have to put that aside.

I look down at the bottles lined up there on the tiled counter.

Just the thought of those pills sticking in my throat, the taste of them going down, slowly dissolving in my mouth as I try to gulp the water down—it's enough to make me want to throw up right now.

I pour the four capsules of the powdered lithium out into my hand. They are an off-colored, sickly pink, glossy, with tiny numbers printed along the center seam.

I put the pills in my mouth and start to swallow, but they seem caught somehow, and I cough and gag as they stick there.

I try again to swallow, but I can't. I can't do it.

I choke and spit the pills out into the sink.

"Goddamnit," I say, gasping, fighting for air.

I grab the already dissolving pills out of the sink and drop them into the trash. Then I open each of the individual pill bottles and empty their entire contents into the toilet. I flush—twice, actually, because they don't all go down the first time.

I splash some water on my face and then turn off the spigot.

"I can't," I tell my reflection, shaking my head. "I can't do it anymore."

I dry my face and hands on a ratty towel hung over the shower.

I switch the light off and close the door.

The medication is gone.

And now I am ready to make things right here—at home—with my family.

Tomorrow I will go to the police station.

I'll talk to Detective Marshall.

And it will be all right.

20.

THE CENTRAL BRANCH OF the San Francisco Police Department is located right on the border between North Beach and Chinatown, in an unassuming two-story building behind a nameless liquor store and directly across from two different strip clubs, Big Al's and the Garden of Eden.

North Beach is maybe my favorite part of the city. It's a little touristy, I guess, but that's just because it's so beautiful. I've never been to Europe, but from the movies I've seen, I think it must look something like the streets here in North Beach. The roads are very narrow, built on the steep, complicated, crisscrossing hills leading up to Coit Tower. The Victorian-style buildings, cafés, and trattorias pressed right up against one another.

There are a few grand old churches, built out of white marble and surrounded by stone courtyards. Before Jane and Teddy were born, my mom and dad lived with me not too far from here. My dad used to take me on walks down around Washington Square Park, and then he'd write at Caffe Trieste while I drew in a notebook and drank hot chocolate and ate these raspberry ring pastry things.

Actually, now that I think about it, once I was older, my dad used to take me and Eliza to that same Caffe Trieste every Sunday to listen to opera music while he worked on his stories for the paper. Walking through North Beach after school—where I basically spent the whole day hiding—can't help but think back on those times with Eliza.

It's only a little after three, but already the sun is low on the horizon, setting behind the high-rise buildings along the Marina to the west. Everything is gray with shadow, and the wind tunnels down the alleyways, blowing the streets clean, as pigeons scurry like rats across the sidewalk.

I light a cigarette, but then throw it away immediately once I see all the cops hanging out around the front of the station—since I'm still under eighteen and could probably get a ticket or something. The cops outside are talking to one another in loud voices, drinking coffee out of Styrofoam cups, their uniforms crisp and polished-looking. Police cars are parked and double-parked all up and down the street.

Inside the station is all cheap tile floors, colorless, threadbare carpeting, and dark-paneled walls. There are posters taped up advertising different police services, along with a bunch of missing person flyers and mug shots. Against the far end of the main room there's a reception desk, where a rather large woman is sitting behind an ancient-looking computer, wearing a bright blue police uniform. There are a couple of wooden benches set up in front of the reception area, but, surprisingly, no one seems to be waiting.

A big cop with a really big mustache pushes past me so I almost fall back.

"Hey, watch it," he says gruffly. "Don't stand in the door."

I take a deep breath and hold it, walking over to the receptionist lady with my eyes fixed on the ground. My heart beats fast and hard.

"Can I help you?" the woman asks, but without looking at me.

The computer screen lights up her broad face, and I can see what must be some kind of spreadsheet reflected in the framed, oversize printout of the department's antidiscrimination policy behind her. She has short silver-gray hair and thick tufted eyebrows and quite a bit of fur on her upper lip. Her mouth is turned down at the corners, and there are deep-set lines around her eyes and crossing her waxen, pale forehead.

"Yes? What is it?" she tries again. "What do you want?"

"I . . . I . . ." My voice trembles, though there's really no reason why it should. I guess I'm just nervous, is all. I'm nervous to talk about Teddy.

"Spit it out, kid, I don't have all day." She speaks in a monotone, still typing at the computer and not looking at me.

"I . . . I . . . I'm here to see . . . Detective Marshall . . . Detective Kerry Marshall."

The woman's head swings back and forth slowly, her eyes fixed on the screen. "Nope. Detective Marshall was transferred to Santa Clara last year."

My breath catches in my throat and, instinctively, I take a step back. "Wh- . . . what do you mean?"

"He was transferred," she says, without any inflection whatsoever. "Detective William Demarest has taken over all of Detective Marshall's cases. Would you like to talk to Detective Demarest?"

"Well . . . I . . . I don't know. Do you . . . uh . . . remember the case of the little boy who went missing from Ocean Beach?"

She keeps typing, still not looking over at me. "Lots of children go missing, I'm afraid."

"Yes, but this was Detective Marshall's case. A boy, Teddy Cole, was kidnapped from Ocean Beach two years ago. It was in all the papers. Teddy Bryant Cole."

Finally the woman stops. She moves her hands off the keyboard and turns to look at me full-on. Her eyes study me. For the first time, there is a hint of color behind the dull gray of her irises.

"Teddy Bryant . . . That case was never solved."

"No," I say timidly. "That's why I wanted to talk to Detective Marshall. Teddy Bryant Cole is my brother."

The woman shakes her head, her lips held tightly together. "I am so sorry," she says. "I am so very sorry for your loss."

My nostrils flare and I grit my teeth.

Teddy is not dead, I want to tell her, but she interrupts me, saying, "I'm sure Detective Demarest will be happy to speak with you. Just wait over there for a moment." She gestures with her head to the empty benches.

I nod. "Yes, okay, thank you."

"It'll just be a moment." And then she smiles again, this time showing off a row of stained yellow teeth.

I sit, waiting on the bench, my legs crossed.

There's a loud noise as the front doors seem to slam open and two police officers, one male and one female, carry a screaming man, hog-tied, through the main entranceway.

"Fucking cocksuckers!" he screams.

Two more men are dragged in the same way behind the first, so all three of them can be heard screaming together.

"Fuckers! Motherfuckers!"

The receptionist woman comes back then, walking just in front of an extremely short man with close-cropped hair and a dark-colored suit and necktie. The man introduces himself as Detective William Demarest, but tells me to call him Bill. I shake his hand and thank the woman, who smiles at me before heading back to her desk.

Detective Demarest—Bill—says that I should follow him, and so I do, walking behind him through a side door and away from those three different hog-tied men screaming profanities.

"I-I'm sorry," I stutter out as we make our way down the cramped hallway past identical windowless offices with different nameplates tacked up on each door. "You must be really busy."

There are trophy cases piled high with different awards and a collection of different badges framed on the yellowed walls.

"Oh, yes, busy, busy, busy," he says in a booming bass voice. "It sure does get crazy in here sometimes. This city's just full of them—crazies, I mean. I've been here goin' on twenty-five years, but I still can't get used to it. Suppose you never do. I thought goin' from homicide to missing persons was gonna be easier somehow. Don't know what the hell I was thinking."

He turns in to the office with his name on the door, and I go in after him.

"Take a seat there," he tells me, pointing to the only chair in the room.

"Ah . . . are you sure?" I ask, considering, as I said, there's literally no other chair in the office.

"Yeah, sit. I'm all right. Here . . ." He pushes some papers onto the floor and moves the lamp and then sits on the corner of the desk so he looks like a little kid, maybe, or like Kermit the Frog, his legs dangling.

Besides the desk and the papers and the lamp and the one

chair, the rest of the office is nothing but filing boxes all stacked one on top of another. The walls are completely blank, and there's not even an inch of free floor space.

"Sit down," he tells me again.

And so I do, holding my backpack on my lap as I lean against the hard metal chair.

"Are you just moving into this office?" I ask dumbly, not sure of what else to say.

He laughs good-heartedly, running his stubby hand through his lack of hair. His nose is very wide, and he has a scar on his chin running straight across like he's been divided into segments.

"You'd think it to look at this place, wouldn't ya?" he says, smiling. "But, no, I've been here a whole year. Took over for Detective Marshall. Did you know him, then?"

"N- . . . no. But he was working on my brother's case."

Demarest nods, still smiling. "Yes, yes. Louise told me. Let's see, I've got the file here. I'm sorry, son; I know your family's been going through a hard time."

He begins rummaging through the boxes of files scattered everywhere.

"Believe it or not," he continues, still riffling, "there's a whole system I got worked out here. I got every case filed just so. Only . . . only sometimes I outsmart myself, you know what I mean? I think myself into a corner. You ever do that, son?"

Standing up straight, he turns and looks at me as though trying to read in my face the answer to his question.

"Nope, nope, I don't figure you do. You're a smart one, I bet, always got everything put back in its proper place. Isn't that so?"

He goes back to looking while I try to say something.

"I . . . I . . . I . . ."

"Oh, that's all right," he tells me. "I've got all the respect in the world for good organizational skills. Now, take that Detective Marshall who was here before me. Why, he kept the most detailed notes I ever read in my damn . . ." He clears his throat. "Darn. Darn life, that's what I mean. And I respect a man like that. I came in here and started reading his case files and, sure enough, it was like reading literature. William Shakespeare. He had a real talent. And organized! Me, I've got my own system. But sometimes—"

"So you read about my brother's case?" I ask, interrupting him this time.

"Sure, of course I did. Tragic stuff."

Emerging triumphant, he lays the surprisingly thin file folder on the table and takes a seat on top of it.

"I've been doing a lot of reading, too," I tell him. "I think my brother might still be alive. That's what I wanted to see you about. That witness, Dotty Peterson, I saw her the other day. She seemed pretty sure that Teddy really was kidnapped."

He frowns at me, his jowls shaking like the gristle on a burned piece of meat. "Ah, yes. Well, the sad truth is, that woman, the witness, she's really not, uhmm, *reliable.* Of course,

I can't discuss too many details of the case, but her story . . . it didn't hold up, not at all."

"What do you mean?"

He pulls the file out from underneath him and begins flipping through it absently. "Well, from what I understand, Detective Marshall had a sketch drawn up of the suspect based on Ms. Peterson's description. Here it is, in fact, right here."

The photocopy of the drawing is in black and white, and I hold it, trembling now, staring down at that face—the face of the man who took my brother.

"What we normally do in a case like this is to both circulate and cross-reference the sketch with our database. These kinds of abductions are almost always perpetrated by sex offenders. So we pulled up every registered sex offender within a thirty-mile radius from the spot the victim, your brother, was taken. Anyone fitting the physical description was immediately brought in for questioning, 'specially if the subject had any contact with the victim. Most times we find the suspects have seen their victims at least once before. Often they've even had some sort of interaction with them. So we cross-check all those different pieces of information. And, from what I can see here, looks like they came back with a list of four possible suspects. Oh . . . and there was the car!"

He says the last part as though surprising himself, pausing to read for a moment before continuing on.

"That's right. That same witness identified a car—a white Ford Explorer. So we ran a check to see if there were any registered Explorer owners on the sex offender list. It looks like there was one relevant match, but . . ."

Grimacing, he turns the papers over one after another.

"From what I can see here, kid, I'm sorry to say, none of the leads panned out in any way. And then, again, just between you and me—I mean, off the record—that witness didn't stand up real well under questioning."

He closes the file, then reaches in his jacket pocket and pulls out a packet of Trident gum. Spearmint, I think.

"Gum?" he asks, holding it up to me.

"No, thank you."

He takes a piece for himself and starts unwrapping it. "Quit smoking a month ago," he says bitterly. He chomps on his gum and finally says, "I'm sorry, I really should be getting back to work. Is there anything else I can tell you, son?"

"No," I answer, bowing my head. "I just wondered if there was anything new, I guess. Do you think I could look at that file?"

"I'm sorry, pal, can't do it. But the truth is, there's not a lot here. The general opinion is that the witness was mistaken. Chances are, Teddy Bryant drowned that day. Ninety-nine-point-ninety-nine percent. I'm very sorry. I wish I had better news for you. If you want, I can—"

But just then another detective sticks his head into the office—a large man with a bald, shiny head, reflecting the buzzing and crackling fluorescent lights overhead. "Hey, Bill, sorry, can I get your signature in here for a second?"

Demarest nods. "Sure thing."

And then to me, "Wait here a second—I'll come walk you out."

He leaves, jumping down off the desk with a thud.

And so I'm left staring at the file.

Drowned, this guy says. But what does he know, really? He's not even the original detective. Plus, this whole place seems a little crazy.

So what I do is, I leap forward and grab the file and tear through it, my heart beating so fast, I can hardly breathe. Sweat breaks out all across my forehead. My vision blurs.

But still, I'm able to find the page with the suspects' names. There are even photos—and what look like street addresses. I take the pages and quickly stuff them into my backpack, closing the file and jumping to my feet, knocking the chair over.

My breathing slows.

I wipe the sweat from my face with the sleeve of my jacket and set the chair to right.

Detective Demarest has not come back, but I leave the office anyway, closing the door behind me.

There is no one in the hall, so I walk quickly out to the main room.

That woman at the front smiles at me and waves.

I go out the door.

No one tries to stop me.

I have the information I need now.

And I will find Teddy.

Because, despite what anyone might say, I know that he is alive.

I know it because I feel it—like a clear, cool breeze blowing through my mind.

PART TWO

21.

OUTSIDE THE FOG HAS settled in over the city, so the streets and skies and buildings and cars and people walking with their heads down and the crows and pigeons and everything are gray and muted silver.

After stealing that list of suspects and being so close to finding Teddy, you'd think the clouds would've parted and the sun would be shining down like a goddamn golden halo all around me.

That's how it would work if this were a movie.

But there is only gray and fog and trash and a thick layer of black sludge ground and beaten into the sidewalk. A bus goes lumbering past, rumbling and shaking, the men and women crowded together inside, sitting and standing.

I run across the street and then go fast up a couple of blocks to get away from the police station, just in case Detective De-marest notices part of my brother's file is missing. Not that he will. He'll stuff the folder back in with all those others as part of his "system." Then he'll forget about it. He'll forget about Teddy, like everyone else has. I'm the only one left who can help him. And so I need to get home as soon as possible to look over what I have.

I hike up the hill to the bus stop on Grant next to Caffe Trieste. I turn to see someone waving at me from inside the coffee shop.

"Miles!"

Of course, it's Eliza. She comes out the swinging door not set right on its hinges.

I say *of course* only because fate or karma or whatever fucking else clearly has it in for me.

So it *has* to be Eliza.

Looking beautiful as always—dark hair pulled back, her face pale, her eyes flashing green-blue against the gray. She's wearing tight jeans and fur-lined boots and a hooded parka. It's cold outside, and she rubs her small hands together.

"Hey!" I say to her, still moving—wanting to get away.

But she immediately starts talking.

And she asks me to sit down.

"What are you doing here?" I ask.

She smiles. "Homework. I'm so far behind."

Those pages I stole are stashed in my backpack, and I want so badly just to go home and read through them. But now Eliza is saying to me, "Come on, Mie. Come sit down for a minute."

I follow her in and order coffee and then I ask her if we can go back outside so I can smoke. She grabs her books and backpack, and we go sit at one of the unsteady tables.

Across the street there is a white church with steeples like pulled sugar stretching up above the white marble steps. There is a pack of street kids huddled together beneath the vaulted arches wearing army gear and wrapped in tattered wool blankets. They have some sort of off-white pit bull mix tied to a long piece of rope.

"Aww, what a cute dog," Eliza says, exhaling the smoke a little theatrically from the cigarette I gave her. "Did you know my mom and I brought a puppy back from New Orleans?"

"Awesome. What kind?"

"A bloodhound," she says, looking down at her hands. "Seriously, they are absolutely the cutest things in the entire world."

Her legs are crossed, and she leans forward. She's very close to me now. I can feel the heat from her body.

I don't want to feel it, but I do.

So I keep on dipping my raspberry ring thing into my big bowl of coffee with sugar and milk.

"Miles," she says, bowing her head. "Listen, I'm really sorry. I didn't mean for it to get out, about what happened. When I came back in I was just upset, and Mackenzie Miller was right there when I told Lily. Remember her? She transferred to Lincoln in eighth grade, and she was totally my best friend."

"Yeah, yeah, of course," I tell her, which is the truth.

"Well, believe me, she wouldn't have said anything, I promise. And I really was too freaked out to notice all the people standing around us. But I think it was Mackenzie. That's what Ian Larkin told me. He said he heard it from her."

I breathe then and drink my coffee. I don't want to care about any of this.

"Look, it's okay. I knew you didn't mean for it to get out."

"Really? Oh, good, Miles. I was worried."

"No, no, I'm fine. And, listen, I hope you know that it had nothing to do with you. I'm on a lot of medication and I get super sick if I don't eat enough. But, anyway, I'm . . . I'm sorry I puked on you."

I smile then, and so does she.

"Well, technically," she starts, stubbing out her cigarette in the red plastic ashtray laid out between us, "you didn't puke *on* me—but you were close."

She giggles sweetly so the table shakes a little and some of her coffee spills into the saucer. A hipster guy in his early twenties walks past, transfixed by the screen of his iPhone—though he still manages to stop and do a kind of double-take when he notices Eliza. He stares and then catches himself staring and averts his eyes back to his phone and keeps on walking.

It's not a big deal or anything.

I mean, it's just a moment—and yet it is enough to remind me that Eliza is really, truly, out of my league.

I swallow and blush and say, "That guy was totally checking you out just then. Did you see that?"

Her head tilts to the side. "What? Who?"

"That hipster dude that walked by. You didn't notice?"

"Uh-uh." She smiles with her lips pressed together.

"I bet that happens to you all the time," I say, maybe because I'm already feeling jealous, which is so totally dumb.

"Yeah, I guess. I'm sort of used to it, you know? Not to sound all full of myself or anything."

I shake my head. "No, no, of course not. It's just a fact, right? You're super beautiful."

But right after I say that, my face goes hot and I'm embarrassed as hell and my heart races and I smoke and don't look at her. It came out sounding really awkward, too.

"No, I'm not." I can hear her fidgeting around. "But thank you."

My throat is very dry. "Sorry, was that weird I said that?"

Her body moves closer to mine.

"No, are you kidding? You're so sweet. Coming back here, I was scared you were going to hate me for what I did. And maybe . . . maybe even blame me for what happened."

I cross my legs and make myself small in my chair.

"Blame you?"

"Yeah, for what happened to you."

"Not all all," I say hurriedly. "Me having that episode . . . I mean, it's a disease—bad wiring in my brain. It's nobody's fault. Nobody's."

She takes another deep breath and exhales noisily. "I know that. But, I don't know, it's just so weird that it happened, like, right after that thing with you and me. Right after I left. I mean, wasn't it after that?"

"Well, yeah, it was. But it's just a coincidence."

She rubs my arm a little. "I wanted to call you after I found out. I really did. Except . . . well . . . like I said, I thought you might be mad at me."

"No, I was never mad at you—not ever."

"I'm so happy to hear that," she says, talking softer now. "I hope we can start hanging out again now that I'm back."

I sit up straight and I'm not sure what to say, but I turn toward her and she's leaning across the table, so I lean in, too, and then we kiss for real this time. Our mouths fit perfectly together, and I taste the warmth and sweetness of her and my body feels lifted off the ground.

We kiss like that until one of those kids from across the street whistles, like, "Woo-hoo," at us.

"You wanna go?" she whispers at me, and I feel drunk or high or both.

We walk down the street together back toward the bus stop, and this time we are holding hands and leaning against each other, and it's so strange because walking to the café we were just friends from long ago running into each other, and now we're, like, a couple.

At least, I think we're a couple.

I kiss her then, as if to ask her, and she kisses me back and she looks up at me and the fog is wet and thick around us and her eyes shine out and she smiles and I know the answer must be yes.

Only . . . only that can't be the answer for me; not yet—not until I bring Teddy back home.

I stop and breathe and press the palm of my hand against my forehead.

"What's wrong?" she asks.

"Nothing," I say. "I just . . . I want this. I do. But . . . I can't. Not right now."

She tilts her head to one side. "But . . . but I thought you were better."

"I am better. But it's not that. I . . . I can't talk about it too much. Not yet."

"What do you mean?"

I start to answer and then stop. As much as I want to talk to her about Teddy, I know that I can't. She would try to stop me. She might even tell my parents. And that's the last fucking thing I need.

None of them will understand. They'll think I'm being reckless. And, anyway, I'm trying to keep them from dealing with the pain of all this. That's the fucking point.

I can't tell her.

So what I say is something completely fucking stupid.

"I just . . . uh . . . need to focus on my own stuff. I'm sorry."

She looks up then, right into my eyes—taking hold of my hands in hers.

"Okay. Yeah, no, I get it."

"You do?"

"Yeah . . . for sure."

The bus lumbers up to the stop and the brakes exhale loudly and the door opens.

It's her bus, the fifteen, not mine.

Eliza gets on board.

"See you tomorrow," she tells me.

The doors close.

And the bus drives off.

22.

THERE'S NO LOCK ON my bedroom door, but that's just the way the house was built; it has nothing to do with me.

I shut myself in and throw my backpack on the unmade bed. The light on the side table has been left on, but it's fully dark outside, so I turn on the overhead light, too, sit down on the bed, and take out the pages.

My hands shake as I try to focus my eyes on the words and images. The photos are black-and-white copies, grainy. My eyes keep watering and I shiver, still not able to see clearly.

"Goddamnit," I say.

I turn the pages over, upside down on the bed, and go up to the computer on my desk, putting on some music to try to calm down a little bit. The library is set to shuffle, and just by chance a John Lennon song plays and it is calming and I go back to the bed.

It's a love song. John's singing, *Even if it's just a day, I miss you when you're away. I wish you were here today, dear Yoko.*

Turning the pages back over, it looks as if the detectives have highlighted the names and addresses of the most likely suspects. The one sex offender on the list who fits Dotty Peterson's description *and* drives a white Ford Explorer lives only three blocks from Ocean Beach, so that seems like a pretty damn good lead. And as I'm reading about the man's alibi— the alibi that cleared him—I notice, unbelievably, that the cops got the date of the actual kidnapping wrong. No wonder Teddy's never been found. These police are seriously incompetent. The date they've written is exactly one week later than the day in question. So the alibi of the man, Simon Tolliver, is totally meaningless.

That breeze comes clear and cool in my mind.

Half the junior class is taking a trip down to Ocean Beach tomorrow to clean up trash. Hopefully I can slip away for a minute to check out Tolliver's house. For all I know, Teddy is there right now.

Reading more about Tolliver, though, I have to admit, I'm a little scared to go confront him. The guy sounds like a total psycho. And while the report states that he's been compliant with his parole officer for almost a decade, he'd been in prison for fifteen years before that.

So he's obviously a bad fucking dude. And honestly, even

though I know I should go and scope out his house, I'm kind of scared about having anything to do with a crazy-ass psycho like that.

But I will.

I'll go there tomorrow and I won't get caught.

There's a Joy Division song now playing on the computer speakers.

And then the door swings open and I jump a fucking mile—turning the pages from the police files over quickly and covering them, as casually as possible, with my backpack.

It's Janey.

She bursts into my room, jumping onto the bed.

"Miles!" she shouts. "That movie was so good!"

I stand up and sit down and knock my bag and the papers back more so they fall off the other side of the bed and onto the ground.

"What movie was it?" I ask, hugging her to me. She smells like clean laundry and maple syrup.

"*Moonrise Kingdom,*" she tells me.

"I wanted to see that. Was it great?"

"So, so great. Where were you, anyway?"

"Nowhere," I answer. "Just walking around."

"We tried calling you."

"Oh, yeah? I guess my phone was off."

I pause for a moment, think, stare at the floor.

"Jane," I say distractedly, "I know things have been hard

around here. But . . . I just . . . It's gonna get better. I promise. I'm going to fix everything."

Her eyes open wide at me. "But everything *is* okay, isn't it?"

"Sure, yeah, of course. But . . . you know what I mean."

She shakes her head. "Don't worry about that."

"No, *you* don't worry. That's what I'm saying."

I am so close now to finding Teddy. This endless hell—this endless waiting—is almost over. I just wish I could tell her. I wish I could tell somebody.

But they will know it soon enough.

When I bring our brother home.

I kiss Jane on the forehead, and we go out together to eat the hamburgers they brought back from Bill's Place on Clement.

The rain is falling outside, and I can hear it like static, loud across the rooftops.

Water drops bead and sweat from the cracked ceiling overhead.

But tonight we eat and we are happy.

Teddy is coming home.

23.

BY LATE MORNING THE rain has stopped.

The school has rented out a bus for us to take down to the beach. It's part of a community service project where each class has to go work somewhere in the city every month. Going to pick up trash at the beach is definitely one of the easier jobs. And thankfully, Eliza's in tomorrow's group, so I don't have to worry about seeing her today.

Preston, too, is in tomorrow's group.

But I do get Jackie with me. We're sitting together on the bus, playing Words With Friends back and forth on her iPhone.

The sky is silvery gray as the sun breaks through the low-lying clouds in places.

Jackie has a hat pulled back on her head and a big parka zipped all the way up to just under her chin. It's seriously cold, and the heat in the bus is broken, so we can see our breath when we talk. I have on a long-sleeve undershirt, a hooded sweatshirt, and my army jacket, but I'm still fucking freezing. The bus rattles and shakes as it snakes down the winding cliff road to Ocean Beach.

I've actually been avoiding coming here ever since Teddy was taken, just 'cause it's been too painful, I guess. The day has replayed in my brain so many times, I didn't want to be forced to think about it any more than I already do. Besides, there are plenty of other beaches to go to north of the city and on the bay.

But now, as we drive along the concrete breaker wall covered in graffiti—the ocean raging loud so we can hear it over the rumbling of the bus's straining engine—I can't help trying to pick out exactly which bathroom I locked myself in and where it was that I last saw my brother—somewhere out on the very edge of the shoreline.

Through the scratched hard plastic bus windows, spattered with mud and smeared with rain not yet dried, the rocky sand and windswept dunes look like images from some postapocalyptic dreamscape. The ocean seems to be moving in every direction at once, waves washing back out to sea from the sloping shoreline so they slam against the incoming breakers and spray up a hundred feet high.

The bus turns into the deserted parking lot past the entrance to the beach on Noriega, and then I become aware that

Jackie has been talking to me for some time now, though I haven't heard one thing.

"What?" I ask, turning back toward her.

She bites down on her lower lip and looks me over. "Weren't you listening to me?"

"Yeah, I was . . . I just . . ."

She laughs at my inability to come up with anything. "Uh-huh. Sure. Are you all right?"

That question again.

Am I all right? Am I all right? Am I all right?

Yes.

Yes, I'm fucking all right. I know I am.

I'm better than all right.

I have hope now. I have hope that Teddy is just a few blocks from here.

And all the rest of it doesn't matter.

"Yeah," I say. "Yeah, totally, I'm fine."

She studies me a little more, as though not convinced.

"Hey," I continue, "would you do me a favor? I've gotta go check something out up on 46th street for a second when we get split up into groups. Do you mind covering for me if anyone asks where I am?"

She remains skeptical. "What are you doing?"

"I just gotta sneak away for a little bit to check something out. It won't take me long."

Her eyes go narrow at me. "Yeah, sure. But what is it?"

There is a moment where I almost tell her. It would be such a relief.

Only I know I shouldn't.

Jackie would worry just like Eliza would. She'd tell my parents and they would freak the fuck out. And then they'd all try to stop me.

I'm sure Dr. Frankel would tell me I'm fucking crazy for even considering doing this. Although he'd say it a whole lot more eloquently than that.

But what he doesn't understand—and what nobody can possibly understand—is that this, doing this now, is the only chance at a sane, healthy life that I'm ever going to have.

So even if this Tolliver guy is a psycho, pedophile, fucking lunatic, I have to face him—and I have to find out. I can't move on with my life until I do. I can't move on until I bring Teddy home. Then I will finally be able to start over.

Telling Jackie is not an option.

So instead I just say, "Nothing. It's a stupid errand I have to run."

"During a school field trip?"

I nod. "Yeah. It'll only take a second."

She brings her shoulders up and then lets them drop again. "All right, Mie, I'll try to cover for you."

"Thanks."

The chance for me to get away doesn't come until after we've already been given gloves and plastic bags and little grabber tools so we don't get stuck with hypodermic needles sifting through the sand. I bring my stuff up behind the public bathroom (not the same one I was in two years ago, I'm pretty sure) and try to hide it all as best I can behind the sea grass growing tall out of the cracked concrete.

I run fast across the Great Highway, dodging cars and not waiting for the light. No one calls after me.

The sky is clearing—or, at least, the sun is breaking through as the south winds blow the covering of clouds and fog farther inland. I put the hood of my jacket up over my head.

Simon Tolliver's house is number 1921 46th Avenue, between Ortega and Pacheco Streets, just three blocks up from the beach. Honestly, it's not what I expected. I guess in my mind I'd made the house up to be some creepy, run-down, dilapidated shack with rusty tools lying everywhere and taxidermy birds hung out front. But it's not like that at all.

Actually, it's a super nice–looking little Craftsman-style home with a pretty vegetable garden in front and a white picket fence surrounding the entire property. There is even a little trellised entranceway covered in purple morning glories and rosebushes in a tangle around the side gate.

It doesn't look like the secret hideout of a deranged kidnapper.

But, then again, maybe he keeps it nice for exactly that reason. A little house like this would be above suspicion.

If he's smart, this is exactly the kind of place he'll live. And he must be smart if he's managed to evade the police for over two years.

The buildings on either side of Tolliver's are bigger, two-story Victorian-style town houses that are separated into upper and lower apartments, so it's impossible to tell whether anyone is at home to see me sneaking around. I decide the best thing to do is just march right up to Tolliver's front door and ring the bell. If he answers, I can always pretend I'm . . . what? Selling magazine subscriptions?

Something like that.

At least that way I'll know for sure whether he's home.

So I let myself in through the front entranceway and take a deep breath, feeling my hands and legs start to shake.

I walk jerkily past the planter boxes of squash and pumpkins and then up the uneven white wooden steps.

I press the buzzer and the doorbell sounds, echoing through the small house.

A dog barks in the distance.

I wait, holding my breath.

But no one comes.

The door remains closed.

Walking, then, slowly around the side of the house, I try to find a window I can see in through, but all the blinds are closed tight. Pressing my face up close to the clouded glass, I can just barely look into what turns out to be the bathroom, but that doesn't help me any. The bathroom is clean. And I can make out the shower curtain printed with a map of the world done up in different colors.

Around the back of the house is a small yard bordered by a row of hedges at least six feet tall. There are patches of green grass, but it's mostly all dead, and the stairs leading down from the back sliding glass doors are all splintered and broken. There is also, in the far corner, tucked up between the hedges and a low-hanging eucalyptus tree, an eight-by-ten-foot wooden shed—the roof covered in leaves and pine needles. The door is fastened shut with a lock, but the lock is left open. There is a dirty window smeared with something built high up on the structure. I can see movement against the glass—flashes of light in the darkness.

I imagine Teddy in there—tied up, gagged, trying to get free.

The clouds are racing past overhead so the shadows sweep across the yard and over the shed in the back, and I can feel my heart beating faster and faster in my chest, my whole body shaking badly so I have to hold my hands tightly together.

I get up to the shed and look in through the window, but it's so dirty, I can't see anything.

There is a noise, though, coming from inside, like newspapers being crumpled together and torn to pieces.

"Hello?" I whisper, pressing my ear up to the crack in the door. "Hello?"

Suddenly there is this feeling I get that someone is looking at me.

I swing around and freeze.

A dog, maybe fifty pounds, like some kind of border collie, is there, inching toward me, growling low and steady.

"H-h-hi, dog," I say dumbly.

The dog growls louder, and I back up against the door of the shed.

"Easy now . . . easy."

I get down on my knees on the damp ground. I avert my eyes and say, "Good dog. Nice, good dog."

Shaking, I extend my hand out so I can feel the dog's hot breath on the tips of my fingers.

The growling stops.

And then the dog's nose presses up cold on the back of my hand.

"Jesus Christ," I say, standing up.

I step back from the door and the dog comes over and lets me pet it for a second.

"Where the hell'd you come from?" I ask.

The dog then goes over to the shed and starts digging and pawing at the ground, whimpering.

I take one last look around before grabbing the lock out of the door and opening it wide.

"Hello?" I say loudly.

The dog goes rushing in ahead of me.

And then a whole shit ton of chickens goes flying and scattering back out.

The dog barks and barks and goes chasing after them, getting one by the neck and shaking it, and I yell, "Fuck!" closing the door just so at least a few of the goddamn things don't get out. I manage to grab a particularly slow-moving chicken, but it pecks at me and squawks so loud, I can't help but let it go again.

The dog, content with its one dead chicken, goes running off. And it's at that exact moment that someone comes around the corner and screams, "Hey, you, stop! What are you doing?"

I turn, startled.

The man is wearing a hooded sweatshirt with the word *Texas* printed in orange letters across it. For some reason, that *Texas* is the only thing I can see. My eyes are fixated on it.

And then he yells again. His accent is thick. "You! What are you doing here?"

My mouth hangs open.

"I . . . I . . ."

I take a step back.

My mind turns round, but comes up with nothing.

"You stay right where you are. Don't move."

"T-Tolliver," I say. "S-Simon Tolliver? I'm looking for Simon Tolliver."

The man stops.

"You knew him?"

"N-no," I stutter. "I . . . He . . ."

The man drops his head. His whole body slumps over like something heavy is weighing him down.

"Did he . . . do something to you?"

I realize, then, that the tears are still coming down, so I wipe my face and try to breathe, saying, "In a way."

"I'm sorry," he tells me, then, coming toward me with his head still bowed, he says, "This Tolliver, he was not a good man. We've been here a few months now. The Realtor told us the story. It's very sad."

My eyes go wide. "He's gone?" I manage to ask. "Do you know where?"

"No. We bought the house from the bank." He clears his throat. "I'm sorry," he repeats.

"It's . . . okay. I'm okay."

And then I turn.

I turn and I run.

The man doesn't call after me.

He lets me go.

24.

THE FOG IS COMING in fast off the ocean, and the wind has gone still. I take my jacket off and wrap it around my waist.

The concrete sidewalk is all busted up from where the roots of trees have grown through, jutting out in places, nature fighting back against the oppressive onslaught of human development.

I take out the picture of Simon Tolliver again and stare into his black-and-white-photocopy eyes.

"What the fuck do I do?" I ask him, waiting for an answer, but getting none.

There's a liquor store on the corner with flashing beer signs in the window, and I go in to get a bottle of water and some peanut M&M's just 'cause I see the package and it looks good suddenly. The man behind the counter looks Korean, with a broad face and thick Coke-bottle glasses.

"Hey," I say, pulling out the photo, maybe for the last time. "Do you know this guy? He ever come in here?"

The man looks lazily at the photo. "Oh, yes, he come here," he says in broken English. "Friday he play lottery."

My breath catches in my throat. "Every Friday?"

He shakes his head. "No. He here last Friday. Lotto, very big. Twenty million. He only come when lotto very big."

I thank him and walk out with the water and M&M's.

The fog is thick, so I can hardly see in front of me. I walk carefully back to the beach.

That cool breeze is blowing through my mind.

I'm getting close.

I can feel it now.

Closer and closer.

Now it's only a matter of time—'til the jackpot gets big enough, 'til I find Simon Tolliver. And Teddy most of all.

25.

THE SKY IS STARTING to clear, so I can see the half pale moon on the horizon. I'm crossing Geary on the way back from having to work a couple hours at Cala Foods, because this other kid, Miguel, called in sick, when I get a text from Jackie, asking if she can come over.

Yeah, for sure, I text her back.

And then I see that I have a missed call from Eliza.

I press the phone to my ear and keep on walking up the street.

Her voice is soft and beautiful through the electronic distortion. She asks me if I want to come over tomorrow night and have dinner with her. She repeats, several times, that she's cool with taking things slow.

Of course, I'm not sure if I should go. I mean, I'm not sure if I should let myself. Finding Teddy is the most important thing, and I'm so close. I can't lose track of that.

But I guess dinner couldn't hurt.

Or, I don't know how it could.

We can have dinner.

And then, when the jackpot's big enough, I'll go back to that liquor store and wait for Simon Tolliver. It's simple, really. And, in this moment, it feels like everything might work out.

So I cross down to Clement Street and walk up to our house.

Jackie is already there, waiting on my front steps, bundled in her giant parka and big knee-high boots.

"Miles, hey, I'm sorry."

I can see she's been crying—her eyes are red and swollen, but not from the cold.

"Are you okay? What's going on?"

She laughs, like it just bursts out of her, then she hugs her knees to her chest and looks down at the concrete.

"A fight," she says.

A fight—with Preston. I take out a cigarette and light it and sit down on the step.

"I'm sorry. Am I bothering you?"

"No, no, not at all. How long have you been here?"

"Just, like, ten minutes." She puts her head on my shoulder. She smells like incense.

"What was the fight about?" I ask.

"I don't know . . . nothing. He's . . . well . . . Does he seem different to you?"

"Different?"

There's yelling from across the street, and I look up to

see two men arguing in front of the Vietnamese restaurant.

"Yeah, different," Jackie says, ignoring the high-pitched shouting. "Like . . . he's so into partying and stuff and . . . I know he's always kind of been that way, but it feels so much . . . *more* now. Does that make any sense?"

"Sure, yeah." I smoke and breathe in and out.

"I'm sorry," she says, taking her hat off and pulling back her long dreads. "I shouldn't be talking about this with you. He's your best friend. It puts you in a bad spot."

I laugh. "Hell, you're my best friend, too. I mean, sometimes I feel even . . . closer to you than—"

"Yeah, me too," she says, cutting me off.

I stare down at the scuff marks on my boots.

"My therapist," I blurt out overly loud. "He tells me this thing about how sensitivity is like a bell curve, you know—like we learned about in school. Basically on one end is someone who's so sensitive they can't even function in the world. And on the other end is, like, a total sociopath, killer, whatever, who can't feel anything. Most people are in the middle—or around the middle. But me, I've always been way closer to the so-goddamn-sensitive-I-can-barely-function side. And I'm not saying you're like that, but you're definitely more sensitive than a lot of people. And . . . and you're a deep thinker, too."

She laughs then. "You don't think Preston is a deep thinker?"

"No, no," I tell her. "It's not that. But he doesn't overthink things. And that's awesome. I wish I could be more like that."

"I'm glad you're not."

She takes my hand in the warmth of hers.

I swallow something down in my throat.

And then my phone vibrates in my pocket.

Jackie lets go of my hand—not that it means anything—and I check the screen.

Again—of course—it's Eliza.

"What's up with her?" Jackie asks, seeing the name on my caller ID.

"Nothin'. She wants me to come to dinner tomorrow night."

"Is that a good thing?"

"Yeah, I guess."

"You going to go?"

"I don't know. I'm not sure if I should. I've been trying to . . ."

Again, I want to tell her about Teddy. But I don't. I can't.

"I'm not sure I have time," I say, hoping that's vague enough.

Jackie kicks the heel of her boot into the concrete.

"Have time? It's one night. I see the way you are, always taking care of everyone. You should go have fun—just do something you want to do."

I smile then and wonder if she's right—or if I can even let myself.

"What about you and Pres? Are you gonna be all right?"

Her eyes close and open. "Yeah, for sure. He's just . . . goin' through . . . I don't even know. Maybe it's 'cause we're comin' up on senior year. And who knows what the hell will happen after high school?"

I nod. "Well, no offense to you or Preston, but I can't wait 'til we never have to see that place again."

She laughs. "Me neither."

I stand and feel a sudden coldness against my cheek. "Come on in," I say. "You had dinner yet?"

I help her up.

"Thank you," she tells me.

We walk together inside.

26.

IT'S AROUND TEN THIRTY when Jackie finally leaves. She stayed and ate dinner with us and watched a couple episodes of *Arrested Development* on Netflix. My mom, of course, took a pill and went to bed. But me and Jackie and Jane and my dad all sat together laughing and eating ice cream. We would've kept on watching probably all night if we could've, but tomorrow's a school day and my dad made us turn it off.

So Jackie gets in her mom's car and drives off, and I say good night to my family and go quickly to my computer. I try to look up the California State Lottery, but, for whatever reason, the page is taking forever to load. There must be something wrong with our Internet.

Anyway, I'm sure the lottery won't be big enough for Simon Tolliver to buy another ticket yet. That guy at the liquor store said it was just at twenty million. Not that I'm 100 percent sure how the whole thing works. I'll have to look it up tomorrow.

I turn the computer off and go to lie down on the bed. But then I hear my phone vibrating again on the table next to me.

It's Preston. His name comes up on the caller ID.

I roll my eyes. I mean, Jesus Christ. Like I'm some couples therapist.

I answer the phone and start pacing around my small room. "Yo. What's up?"

His voice comes through strained. "Did you talk to Jackie?"

"Yeah, she just left here."

"Oh." There's a pause, then, "Is she okay?"

"Yeah, of course."

Another pause. "Can I come over for a second, you think? Smoke a cigarette?"

"You don't smo—"

"Come on," he cuts in. "Please. I don't have anyone else to talk to about this stuff."

I nod my head, though obviously he can't see that. "Sure, yeah, no problem," I say.

He thanks me over and over.

We hang up.

It's funny, I guess.

And I'm happy, too, that I'm able to be here for him—for both of them. As they've always been there for me, no matter

what. So I put on my big jacket and a hat and a scarf and these
fingerless gloves, 'cause it really is cold outside. I have old-
fashioned-looking plush slippers that used to be my dad's, so I
put those on, too, and grab my pack of cigarettes.

Out in the kitchen, my dad is up still, boiling water on the
stove. He's wearing a bathrobe over flannel pajamas and drinking a glass of straight whiskey.

"What's up, Tiger? Can't sleep?" I say to him, and he laughs.

"That's right, old man. What about you?" he says.

"Preston called. He's coming over."

"You're the marriage counselor tonight, huh?"

"That's just what I was thinking."

"You want some hot chocolate?" he asks.

I smile at him. His beard has grown in thick and long, so he
almost looks like some hipster guy from the Mission.

"Is that what you're having?"

He nods.

The kettle starts to whistle on the stove, and my dad turns
the flame off.

"You're a good friend," he tells me.

And then my mom yells from their room, "Sam! What are
you doing?"

I guess maybe the kettle woke her up.

"You better go on out," my dad whispers.

I do as he says.

The night is very black and very cold—none of the streetlights are working, and the wind is still blowing in strong from across the bay. I smoke my cigarette and wait for Preston's little Fiat to pull up in front.

He arrives about a minute later.

"My man," he says as we hug briefly. He smells, as always, like pot and incense. His ski jacket is zipped all the way up to his chin, and he has a wool hat pulled down low over his eyes. "It's fucking freezing."

I nod. "Sorry, my mom's up," I tell him. "You mind if we sit out here?"

"Of course, yeah. That was the plan."

He leans against the railing, and I crouch down on the balls of my feet.

"Jackie said she came over here."

I scratch at the back of my neck. "Oh, so you talked to her?"

He scratches at his broad chin with long, thick fingers, the nails wide and flat. Above him a large crow flies down from the branches of a scraggly-looking beech tree. I blink my eyes to try to make it disappear, but it's still there, hovering in midair.

"We texted," he says. "What, you guys had dinner or something?"

"Yeah. We watched *Arrested Development*. She was upset."

I blink again and watch as the crow swoops down lower. I tell myself it must be in my head. It has to be. It's the middle of the night.

But then the crow flies up again. It flies up, and a giant

glob of white crow shit goes splattering all over the shoulder of Preston's jacket.

"Jesus! What the hell?"

"That bird took a shit on you," I say.

"Jesus Christ."

"I mean, what are the fucking chances?"

He laughs and I laugh and we laugh together.

"Look, man," I say after a minute. "I get you coming over here. But Jackie loves you. Seriously, you don't have to worry."

Preston crouches down next to me. "Really? She's okay?"

I nod. "Of course. She loves you."

He smiles and plays with the zipper of his jacket. "It's that simple, huh?"

"It seems like it, yeah—though obviously I don't know anything about relationships."

"What? Yeah, you do."

"I know about fucking them up."

He spits over the railing. "What does that mean?"

"You know what it means."

"Eliza? That wasn't your fault."

My eyes close. "No, that's not it."

"Then what, man?"

"Nothing," I tell him. "It's nothing."

He puts his hand on my shoulder. "Well, anyway, I appreciate you lettin' me come over like this."

"Of course."

He smiles. "I should probably hang out with Jackie tomorrow night. But maybe Saturday we can all go to a movie. Are you gonna try to see Eliza?"

I smile back. "Yeah, I guess I am."

He nods. "Well, be careful, okay? You're probably sick of me saying it—but be careful."

"Thank you. I will."

"You better."

We hug and say good-bye, and he starts down the stairs.

"Sorry about that crow shit," I call after him.

He gets in the car.

And drives away.

27.

ELIZA'S FAMILY HAS MOVED into a new house since I knew her last—and, from what I can tell from here at least, it's a lot smaller than I would've imagined.

She points it out to me—a two-story town house at the top of the park at Alamo Square, a tiered park with a view of the entire downtown skyline and the Bay Bridge and the East Bay in the distance.

We hike up the concrete steps that cut through the center of the park, passing the playground we used to play in together when we were kids. There's something so familiar being here with Eliza, and in a way, it's like no time has passed at all.

The sky is clear and cold and the wind blows in strong off the ocean. As we walk through the park together, I look out and can see the reflection of the sun on the windows of the houses along the East Bay like fire spreading.

Eliza says nothing, but takes my hand in hers, and I feel her warmth against the wind and the cold. She has the hood of her sweatshirt up covering her hair and is wearing a heavy jacket over her sweatshirt and those same torn jeans tucked into big lace-up boots. Her eyes are very blue against the black of her hair and the fading light.

She leans forward then, and I realize she's trying to kiss me and so I drop the backpacks and I kiss her and she kisses me, and the feel of her against me makes me dizzy and light-headed.

"This is me taking it slow," she says, her nose pressed against mine.

I don't have it in me to fight her. Not when I've spent what feels like my whole life chasing after her.

We kiss, our mouths and tongues together, and we breathe into each other, and it's like everything in my life has been leading up to this exact moment. It is all perfect, part of some greater plan for me and for her and for the whole universe. We are kissing and it is all beautiful and miraculous and exactly as it's supposed to be—like there really is some divine will looking out for me, looking out for us both.

I put my hand on her tiny waist, beneath her jacket and sweatshirt and T-shirt, and feel her warm skin, and she shivers against me. I put my other hand on the small of her back and she seems to fall into me, and I kiss her and she kisses me and I'm flushed and shaking—and then she pulls away, saying, "Come on, let's go inside."

I kiss her again.

"Come on, let me show you around inside."

I pick up the two backpacks—mine and hers.

She takes my hand.

And now we walk together.

28.

CHRISTINA, ELIZA'S MOM, IS a pretty good chef, just like Eliza's dad—though she's not a professional or anything.

She makes us these amazing-looking grilled cheese sandwiches and a salad with roasted corn cut off the cob and cherry tomatoes.

She has black hair and green-blue eyes like Eliza's, though her features are much more narrow and petite. She wears a long shapeless dress and a necklace with a jagged crystal hanging from the end.

She's an old-school hippie. She always has been. She's into the whole organic, local food movement and everything.

But, like I said, her food is awesome.

She puts the sandwiches down in front of us, and Eliza asks if I want a beer.

"You drink beer now?" Christina asks me, and I hesitate before saying, "Uh, yeah."

Mother and daughter exchange glances, and then they both smile.

"Well, what the hell?" Christina says. "I'll have one, too."

She gets out three bottles of this apricot-flavored Pyramid ale, and I feel very adult suddenly. We're all sitting together in their giant kitchen with brand-new appliances and high ceilings, and it almost feels like me and Eliza are this grown-up couple in an apartment we live in together.

The table is made up of mosaicked tile, and the colors are vibrant. I realize I'm kind of staring when Christina says, "It's good to see you, Miles. It's just like old times, no? Cheers."

She holds out the beer and we all "cheers" together, and I look over at Eliza and she's smiling back at me.

"By the way," Christina continues, "we're going to Carmel for Christmas. I've rented a suite for the week. You really should come."

Arrow, their one-year-old bloodhound, is currently positioned under my chair, trying to get whatever scraps of food I might be able to give him. He obviously assumes, since I'm the new guy, that I won't know the rules about no scraps from the table. And I guess he's right, 'cause I sneak him a corner of my sandwich and he slobbers all over my hand eating it.

"Remember when we'd go up to Tahoe when you were kids?" Christina asks me. "That was such fun."

"Of course." I look over to Eliza to get her approval. "Are you sure that would be all right if I come?"

"Totally," she says cheerfully.

"Then it's settled. It'll be our treat."

Christina drinks down more of her beer, and so I do, too.

"Liesy's so happy to be back," she says. "She's thrilled to see you again."

I drop my head, blushing a little.

"It broke my heart to see you two leave on such bad terms. And I am so sorry to hear about all the trouble you've had."

I nod my head slowly, breathing out. "Yeah."

"It's not fair. This kind of thing always happens to the sweetest people. But you're in good company. Madness and genius are very closely related, you know?"

"Yeah, right. I'm the last thing from a genius."

"Well, you are a sensitive soul. The world needs more people like you. Lord, compared to that Neanderthal Liesy was with in New Orleans—"

"Mom!"

I see Eliza's face go flushed even more, and she has her eyes open wide like she's trying to communicate with her mom through facial expressions.

"I'm just saying. You are a major improvement."

Eliza keeps on staring her mom down. "Mom! Please." Then she turns to me. "She is right, though. You are an improvement."

I fidget some. "Gee, thanks . . . I guess."

Eliza smiles now and looks at me very sweetly.

We look at each other for a few moments just not saying anything. I have this intense urge inside of me to tell her I love her. I mean, I know that's crazy since we haven't even really spent any time together in over two years. But, then again, this whole thing is crazy. It all feels so . . . so meant to be . . . so natural. Like some guiding force brought us back together.

"Oh, aren't you guys cute!" Christina says, clasping her hands together.

Eliza and I both blush and look down.

"It's perfect," she continues. "Oh, Miles, by the way, I want you to write down your birthday and, most importantly, your birth time for me before you go. I want to do your charts, okay?"

"You mean, like, astrology?" I ask.

"Yeah," Eliza says, rolling her eyes. "Mom's super into that these days. It is kinda cool, though. You'd be surprised how right on the readings are."

Christina smiles. "Well, of course they are. The planets control the tides, don't they? Human beings are seventy-five percent water; it makes perfect sense the planets would control us, too."

I nod politely. "Wow, yeah, I never thought of it that way."

"It'll be fun to see what it says about us," Eliza tells me.

Christina leans forward on her elbows. She's wearing a cardigan sweater over her dress, and there's a strange brooch, like some kind of amulet, pinned over her breast.

"My guess is you two have been doing this for many lifetimes together, over and over. Otherwise how could you have possibly found each other so young?"

"Mom, please."

"I'm sorry, dear. You're right. It's not good to talk too much about these things. I do have a tendency to overanalyze everything. Are you spending the night, Miles?"

The question startles me a little, and I choke, coughing. I mean, God, how I want to. And, God, how I don't want to tell them the truth, that my mom would probably freak the fuck out if I asked her. She thinks me seeing Eliza again is going to mean me going batshit crazy again—maybe hurting Jane this time like I hurt Teddy last time.

But I do want to stay. I want to stay so badly. Everything here is just . . . just exactly the way it should be. I think about that Washington Phillips record. It seems so strangely coincidental that I would be listening to all this gospel music and suddenly it's as if there really is a power like God in my life.

There is that cool breeze blowing through my mind, and I feel as if there might actually be a power coming to take away all my pain and suffering and the suffering of my family. I'm not sure how that's going to happen. But it *is* going to happen. I will be with Eliza and I will find Teddy.

My mom will be upset at first. But soon she'll come to see. She'll come to understand.

I swallow and look up at Eliza.

"I'd really like to," I say.

"Good," Christina says. "Because you're welcome any time. It feels good having a man around the house again, doesn't it, sweetie?"

Eliza smiles and blushes some more and shakes her head. "Yeah, Mom, Jesus. That's enough, all right? Come on, Miles, you want to go outside?"

"Yeah, sure."

I take my plate over to the sink, and then Eliza and I head out to the front porch to smoke.

That breeze is there, cool and gentle and calming.

I open the door.

We both step outside.

29.

THE PORCH IS PAINTED a dark red color, and we sit on the top step. There is no one on the street and no cars driving past.

"I'm sorry my mom is so intense," Eliza says, dragging on her cigarette. "She means well."

I kiss the back of her neck and her lips and she tastes like apricot beer and cigarettes. I wrap my arms around her and hold her close.

The wind is blowing the fog in around us, so we are covered in this blanket of mist and it grows ever thicker. We are alone in the middle of a dream. There is nothing but the fog and Eliza and me, and whether I say it or not, I know we are in love, that this is love, an ancient soul love that was given to us by a power greater than either one of us.

We kiss and are lifted up together.

The fog carries us away into the night.

Nothing can touch us.

We are sacred.

We are chosen.

Her body is pressed against mine, and it's like I can't get close enough, like I want to stitch my skin together with hers so we are together like this forever.

I thank God.

I say it out loud: "Thank God."

Her eyes sparkle in the damp.

This is heaven.

Right here and now.

30.

THE SUN STREAMS IN bright through the window in the morning, and I turn and see that she really is still there next to me. Eliza is there. I mean, she's here—sleeping, curled on her side, wearing a white tank top and underwear.

It's very early still and there are birds chirping loudly from the surrounding rooftops. Eliza seems to be sleeping heavily, but when I kiss her cheek she blinks her eyes awake.

All around us the room is white and clean and perfect, and the bed is white and soft, and she leans forward to kiss me and we kiss together and she tastes clean and perfect and I close my eyes and we kiss more. Her body is so soft and warm beneath my hands and beneath my body, and I kiss her all around her neck and shoulders. She makes little noises, and so I keep going and kiss down her body around the softness of her belly and her hips jutting and down the heat of her thighs.

"Is this okay?" I whisper.

And she whispers back, "Yes."

"Are you sure?"

"Yes, yes," she says. "I'm sure."

She seems so tiny underneath me, and I kiss her for what feels like hours, and the room fades out all around us and the walls crash down and it's like we are floating there, and then we make love and it is more perfect and pure and incredible than anything I could've ever imagined, or ever dreamed.

When it is over we lie together intertwined like that and we breathe heavily, and then finally . . . finally . . . we fall back to sleep. Or I do, anyway.

I fall asleep.

And I dream.

I dream that I am at the beach.

At Ocean Beach.

But the tide is so low, I have to walk for what seems like miles and miles to the water. The sun is bright and warm like the day Teddy went missing.

I walk out, trying to reach the ocean, and suddenly I see him, standing there with his back to me. His red hair is shaggy, and he's wearing those same floral-patterned board shorts and the same loose-fitting T-shirt.

He is walking toward the ocean, too, and I am walking behind him, and I call out, "Teddy! Hey, Teddy!" But he doesn't answer or turn back toward me.

I keep calling and calling.

He won't turn around. He won't turn around or acknowledge me.

And as I run to try to catch up, he just keeps getting farther and farther away.

Until finally he is in the ocean.

I yell, "Stop, Teddy, come back!" Getting more and more frantic.

It does no good.

He disappears beneath the waves.

I scream.

Then all at once my legs begin sinking into the sand. The sand is like quicksand, pulling me under. I sink down to where my chest and lungs are compressed from the pressure of the entire beach closing in around me. I sink down.

And then I hear it.

The voice.

The voice from the bathroom that day at the beach.

The sound of it makes me want to pull my skin off and scream so there's nothing left inside me.

"*Miles*," it says, whispering—eating through my brain. "*Miles, stop. Stop fighting. This is what you want.*"

"N-no," I gasp, but then the sand covers me.

I close my eyes and there is only this intense heat and this crushing feeling and I can't breathe.

And then I jerk awake.

It is late, I can tell right away—the afternoon sun warm and orange-colored.

Eliza is still next to me, but there's this sick feeling in my stomach. I'm not sure why the hell her mom didn't wake us up for school. I stagger to the bathroom and run the faucet and try to get the world to stop spinning.

That voice from the dream is still there, whispering at the back of my mind.

I thought it was the voice of some power like God guiding me toward Eliza. But it is the opposite of that. It was tricking me. It made me forget. It made me spend the night here instead of going home, like I should've, to be with my family. They need me. Teddy needs me.

This, with Eliza, it is a distraction.

It's going to make me hurt the people I love.

I lied to my mom and dad. I told them I was spending the night at Preston's. How could I have done that? I see it so clearly now. After everything I put them through, this is such a betrayal.

My heart is beating fast now, so it's almost painful in my chest.

I go back to Eliza's room and start putting my clothes on.

"What . . . Where are you going?" she asks, sitting up.

"I have to get out of here," I say, my voice shaking. "I'm sorry. I shouldn't have stayed."

She pulls the covers up around her. "What do you mean?"

"Nothing. I'm sorry. It's not . . . It's me. It's my fault. This is all my fault. I'm sorry. Once I find him, once I make it right, then we can be together. But I shouldn't be here now."

"I can't believe this is happening," she says, but like she's talking more to herself, the sobs choking her, the tears coming down.

"I'm sorry."

I put on my shoes then, fast, and start toward the door.

"Miles, wait," she calls.

But I can't wait. I can't.

I have to get out.

I have to get out right now.

And so I run down the stairs and out into the warmth of the afternoon sun. The wind has died down. The city is still and shimmering in the soft light.

This was a mistake, but I will make it right.

I will tell my family.

And I will make it right.

That voice is there whispering in my mind again—but it is different now.

"Stay away from her," it tells me. *"Stay away."*

It tells me that until I find Teddy, I can't have anything to do with her.

Being with Eliza, that was a test. I almost got sucked in— drowned in the quicksand.

But I got out.

And now I'll go off to school—even if I'm late. And it will all be all right.

Soon I'll have Teddy back. And the voice will be silenced. And maybe then I will get to be with Eliza again.

But for now, that doesn't matter.

Nothing does.

Except for my family.

Except for Teddy.

31.

"YOU WHAT?" MY MOM yells. "You spent the night at Eliza's? And you missed more than half the day at school?"

She and my dad are standing there together.

"Were her parents there, at least?" my dad asks.

"Her mom was, yeah."

The sun is low over the trees of the Presidio, and the house is all dark gray, covered in shadows.

"Why did you lie to us, Mie?" my dad asks again.

My mom cuts me off before I can answer. "What difference does it make why? He lied to us. After everything. Jesus Christ."

"Mom, I'm sorry."

I sit down on the couch then and notice Jane watching us from her room. I say, "I know I screwed up. I know it. But I'm gonna make it right. I promise."

"How can you?" my mom yells. "You can't. You can't make it better. You lied to us. All we do is worry about you, and you lied to us. It's unforgivable."

My dad sits down on the couch next to me and puts a large hand on my shoulder. "No, no. It's okay."

"No, it's not okay!" my mom yells. "Sam, don't tell him it's okay. I'm sick of you always making me be the bad guy."

My dad sighs loudly. "Sweetie, that's not it. He told us, didn't he? He knows he shouldn't have lied."

"But he did," my mom says. And then, turning to me, "You did lie. That's the point. It's unacceptable."

"You're right," I tell her. "Mom, you're right. I'm not arguing with you. And I'm so, so sorry. I promise you, I'll never do it again."

My mom gets right in my face. There are tears in her eyes—and in mine, too.

"Why should I believe you? *How* can I believe you?"

"I'm sorry," I say dumbly.

She sits down next to me on the couch, buries her face in her hands—and cries and cries.

"It's all right," my dad whispers, putting his hand on her back. "Please, sweetie, it's all right."

"I'm sorry," I tell them both. "I'm sorry, I'm sorry, I'm sorry."

My mom continues to cry.

"I just . . . ," she says through her tears. "I can't take it."

Bringing my knees up to my chest, I rock back and forth slightly on the couch.

"I'll make it up to you," I whisper, more to myself than to them. And then, louder, "I'll make it better. I promise. I'll make it all better."

"It's okay," my dad tells me. "Why don't you go to your room for a little while?"

"I'll make it up to you," I say again.

"Please," my dad repeats.

I stand up and walk to my room.

And I leave them all where they are—better off without me.

32.

IT'S AN HOUR OR so later when I go back out in the living room. My mom and dad and Jane are all watching some black-and-white movie on TV I can't place, but Jane gets up from the couch when she sees me and comes to give me a hug, and I kiss the top of her head.

"Hush," my mom says. "Come on, quiet, this is the good part."

She's referring to the movie, and I suddenly recognize it as *To Kill a Mockingbird* with Gregory Peck—the courtroom scene.

"Sorry," I whisper.

Me and Jane go over to the couch, and I lie on the floor and watch the movie. And even though I know they're all mad at me, it's nice being here—home—with my family.

Jane holds my hand as we watch. Gregory Peck gives a speech, and there is Scout, and I inhale the familiar smell of our house, along with the Christmas tree they must've put up after school yesterday, while I was gone. It's scraggly and an off color, with soft yellow lights and a few varied ornaments. My dad is on the couch with Mom, and he's sipping a drink and she's leaning against him.

This is my family, and I love them more than anything.

Curling on my side, I take my jacket off and cover myself like it's a blanket.

There is a commercial now, and the local news anchor flashes on-screen. "Ninety-five-million-dollar-historic-high-for-the-lotto-jackpot-more-news-at-eleven," he says.

The tears burn my eyes and I cry softly.

I cry because I'm happy.

"I'm going to make this right," I say aloud.

My dad rubs my back with his big, callused hand.

"I'll make it right, I swear."

33.

THE BUS BRAKES SUDDENLY and I'm thrown forward into the hard plastic seat in front of me. A large man with a sunken, grizzled face turns and glares at me.

"Sorry," I say.

He doesn't answer. The light is gray and dull through the scratched windows.

I pick up my book off the floor and continue trying to read.

My eyes can't focus, though. The words blur out, and I just keep thinking over and over how perfect this all is.

Everything, my whole life, it has all been leading to this moment—today, right now.

The bus rattles down the highway, becoming slowly more and more engulfed in the fog.

In order to get down to Ocean Beach before work gets out, I

did have to cut my last two classes. But when I come back with Teddy, I'm sure everyone'll be quick to forgive me.

Because I am going to find Teddy.

It will all come full circle. It's so clear to me.

That voice is there like a gentle wind—telling me that I will find him.

"You're going to find him. You're going to make it all better."

I get off the bus at the stop near the liquor store. The fog is thick and heavy, but it's still warm. The heat surges through me as my lungs expand and contract and my hands shake badly trying to get a cigarette lit.

The liquor store is just a block up, and I walk it slowly, going over and over the not-very-well-conceived plan I've put together. Not that it matters. I don't need a plan. The voice, the power, will see me through this. But I do need to find a good spot to wait for Tolliver without drawing too much attention to myself.

Everything is pretty empty, at least at the moment—two thirty on a Friday afternoon—but I figure once school and work get out there'll be more people. Besides the liquor store on the corner, there's a KFC catty-corner and an auto shop right next to it. Across the street is an old travel agency that looks like it's been closed since the nineties. Frisco Travel, that's what the sign reads. There's also a check cashing place next to that, and I watch a very slow-moving old man walk, bent and pained, out the swinging plate-glass doors, through the fog, to his silver Buick sedan.

A black-and-white cat with a bell on its neck darts quickly up the block and cuts through a side alley.

I drag on my cigarette and keep my attention focused on the liquor store.

A pickup truck, shiny and new-looking, pulls into the lot, and a very tall, very skinny man with big brown boots steps down onto the gray asphalt. It is not Simon Tolliver.

I get ready to wait.

The waiting seems to go on and on.

But that wind blowing in my mind makes me feel at peace all through my body. I am exactly where I am supposed to be. I don't just believe that, I *know* that right down to the center of me.

So I sit smoking and watching the entrance to the liquor store.

Hours pass.

I go inside once to buy a water, a Starbucks drink, and some of those pink-and-white animal cookies. The clerk is that same Korean guy, but he doesn't seem to recognize me.

Outside I eat the cookies and sit on the curb. The fog gets thicker and thicker as the sun begins to set and the world turns dark around me. But still, I sit and wait.

The time goes by.

And then I see it.

A white Ford Explorer—the same kind of car Dotty Peterson saw Teddy getting into.

It pulls into the parking lot and the man gets out. There's no question: It is Simon Tolliver.

He's tall and very thin, with a bald head and glasses. He wears a barn coat over a hooded sweatshirt, with his jeans tucked into knee-high rain boots. Dirt is splattered across his chest, and he's got on a pair of cracked leather gloves, though, like I said, it's really not cold out.

He walks with his head down into the store.

"*Now*," the voice whispers.

I run over to his car and try to find anything suspicious-looking inside. I know I don't have a lot of time. My heart is beating fast and my eyes can't seem to focus. I breathe. There are tools in the way back and a tarp, so quick as I can, without really thinking too much, I open the trunk and climb inside, slamming the door shut and crawling under the tarp. Almost instantly I hear the front door open, and the man gets in. I hold my breath, waiting for him to find me—to throw the tarp back and murder me right there—but he doesn't. He starts the engine and some twangy old-fashioned country music plays softly.

I feel the car lurch backward and turn.

Wherever the hell he's going, I'm going with him. There's no turning back now. I curl up tight and try to hold on to that voice, that cool breeze in my mind. That voice will tell me what's right. It will protect me.

The car hits a bump and I slam against the back of the seat and the tools rattle all around me.

But, as far as I can tell, Tolliver still doesn't know I'm here. I check my phone in my pocket then, to make sure it's on silent. There are three missed calls from my dad and one from

Eliza. Obviously, I can't listen to them now. My dad's probably worried about me, wondering where I am. Mom probably told him to call me. They'll both be really angry. But when they see I have Teddy, that I rescued him, of course they'll forgive me.

I grab on to a very large rusted metal wrench to use as a weapon in case I need to fight my way out. The voice whispers softly to me that I am being taken care of—that it will not abandon me. And so I lie still.

34.

WE DRIVE FOR A LONG, long time before the car finally pulls off onto what feels like a dirt road. I bump around in the back for a while until finally the car comes to a complete stop and Tolliver kills the engine and I hear the door open and slam.

There's the steady sound of crickets chirping. I pull back the tarp. The night is dark. Only the light from a little farmhouse illuminates the field of artichoke and burned-out tractor parts scattered everywhere.

Crawling over to the backseat, I switch the overhead light so it won't come on, then I open the door and climb out, easing the door shut behind me.

From what I can see, I must be on a working farm up on the cliffs. There's heavy fog and the sound of an owl in the distance.

Running hunched and low, I creep around the side of the

house. There's a woodpile built up next to one of the windows so I climb up and try to see in through the drawn curtains. All I get is the corner of maybe the living room. There's a hardwood floor and a yellowed wall, but that's all I can make out.

And then there's a shadow and the voice of a little boy, around ten years old.

"No, no," he calls out.

Tolliver stumbles into the room and grabs hold of him. "Come on. It's okay."

He carries the boy back, and for a moment I can see the two of them perfectly silhouetted.

Tears come to my eyes and I take a deep breath.

It is Teddy.

I thank God.

It is Teddy and I've found him and everything is going to be all right.

I reach into my pocket to get my phone to call the police.

But my phone isn't there and I realize it must've fallen out in the car somewhere.

I run back and begin rummaging around amongst all the tools and things. The phone is there and I open it frantically, but there's no signal way out here on this farm.

I can't believe I'm even thinking this, but the only thing to do is go in there myself. So I grab that same rusted wrench and hold it tightly in my hand. I start toward the house, breathing heavily.

But then there is a light coming from over the dirt road in the distance and I watch, openmouthed, as the light gets closer. Another car. It's almost right on top of me before I can move—but I do, I move, running behind the corner of the house, crouching down low.

The car is a black sedan, and a man walks out quickly, wearing a big coat, carrying a black leather-looking bag. He goes to the front door and knocks. Tolliver lets him in a second later.

I climb back up on the woodpile and wait.

The man that's come in has a really low voice and I hear him shouting, "Hold him down. Hold him down there."

My throat swells, and I feel the adrenaline surge through me—rushing straight to my brain.

I climb down.

I hold the wrench tightly in my hand and run round to the front door.

I grab hold of the door handle and pull it open. There's a strange musky smell in the house, and it's dimly lit. The sound of voices comes from my left, and I take a deep breath and run headlong into the room. I have the wrench raised up over my head. I can't even hear because my heart is beating so fucking loud. I shake and scream and run in and feel heat all through my body.

"Let him go! Let him go!" I yell as loud as I can.

Tolliver turns first and grabs my wrist, and his hand is

fucking strong and he shakes my arm so the wrench falls, and then I swing my other hand and hit him in the face.

"Ah, what the hell?" he shouts.

The other man, with the deep voice and dark features, grabs me from behind and throws me on the ground.

I hit the hardwood floor and sit up, and then I look over on the couch and see Teddy is there, with a cloth on his head. I try to stand up, but the deep-voiced man pushes me down again.

"Call the police," he yells to Tolliver. "I'll hold him here."

"No, I'll call the police," I yell louder. "Teddy. Teddy, it's me!"

The deep-voiced man leans over me, pinning my arms back. "Stop it. Who are you? What are you talking about?"

Then Teddy shrieks and vomits on the rug next to me.

Tolliver comes running to help Teddy up.

"Christ, Doc, he's so sick. You gotta help him."

The man he called Doc looks up at Tolliver, carrying Teddy. "What about this kid?"

"I'll take care of him. Here, help me."

Teddy cries again, then he throws up all over his T-shirt.

"Jesus," I say. "Teddy! What'd you do to him?"

The man, Doc, gets up off me and takes Teddy in his arms.

"Kid," Tolliver says, shaking me by the shoulders, "there's no Teddy here. My boy is sick. Can't you see that? You better get out of here."

"Your boy?" I keep on yelling. "He's my brother! You kid-napped him!"

"Simon!" Doc calls from the bathroom.

I try to find the wrench, then, on the ground, but somehow it's not there anymore. Tolliver goes off to the bathroom and I race to follow him.

The noise of the water is very loud.

"Kid," he says, "I don't know what you're talking 'bout. My boy—my son—is sick."

Teddy is stripped and lying in the bathtub as the water fills around him. His eyes are nearly shut and his face red and sweaty, though at the same time he is shivering from the cold.

"That's my brother! That's Teddy! What did you do to him? Teddy!"

Tolliver gets my wrists and shoves me into a sitting position on the tile, and Doc comes over and points his finger right in my face.

"Who are you?" he demands. "What are you doing here? Listen to me, *there is no Teddy here.*"

Tolliver then grabs me by the wrists again and yanks me to my feet. "See? This is my son, Colin. He's real sick."

I stare at Tolliver, and—I see a genuine kindness in his dark eyes. He has a big broad face and is just big and broad in general. His skin is a reddish brown, and he has large hands with long fingers. He places one of those hands gently on my shoulder.

"Kid, you are obviously confused. Why don't you start at the beginning and tell us who you are."

I stammer, so goddamn frustrated now I can't fight the tears back. "My brother, he was kidnapped two years ago from Ocean Beach and now he's here. You have him."

Tolliver shakes his head, but his eyes soften and I see something like pity there.

"Kid," he starts. "Kid, come on, take a look at my son. Take a good look. Slow down. Breathe. And look. This is Colin. My son."

My shoulders drop, and I do what he says. I look at Teddy through the blur. I rub my eyes and look again.

The boy has turned pale and his lips are bluish purple and he's shivering terribly. His hair is matted down and greasy—his dark brown hair, his large forehead, his thin, trembling lips.

Dark brown hair.

It is not Teddy.

He doesn't even resemble Teddy—not really.

Teddy is a redhead with freckles. Teddy's nose was broken when he was six, and it's been crooked ever since. Teddy has a wide mouth and big green eyes.

I put my hands on the edge of the bathtub and try to steady myself. The tears come so I can hardly breathe.

"It's not him," I cry. "It's not Teddy."

Simon Tolliver puts his arm around me.

"Hey, it's okay," he says. "I remember now. That case. The kid who was kidnapped at Ocean Beach two years ago? Teddy . . . uhmm . . . Bryant? Was that it?"

"Uh-huh," I say. "Teddy Bryant Cole."

"But what made you think he was here?" the doctor asks, working at the boy's—not Teddy's—forehead with a cloth.

"The . . . the police report," I whimper. "You were the last chance I had."

I feel Tolliver's hand rubbing my back and I want to go home suddenly, so goddamn badly.

"It's okay," he says. And then he turns to the doctor. "Doc, you don't know this about me, but I had a real . . . troubled past. I was in prison and . . . I did some bad things. But I've changed. I went to counseling, I met Cheryl. I turned my life around. It's been years now." And then to me, "But I promise you, kid, I had nothing to do with that boy's disappearance. The police questioned me. I didn't do anything."

The doctor clears his throat. "We don't have time for this. You go get those clothes and a bag together. And get a blanket to wrap Colin in. He's ready. We need to leave immediately. None of that matters now." He leans over and pulls the drain from the tub.

"Yeah, okay. Thanks, Leo," Tolliver tells him. "We'll get you taken care of, too, kid, don't you worry," he says to me.

He leaves then, and the doctor grabs a few white towels off the rack.

Rubbing the boy's body roughly with the towel, he contin-ues talking, murmuring through gritted teeth. "Don't know what you were thinking, bursting in like that. It's a good way to get yourself killed. You're damn lucky you came in here when

Colin was so sick. Simon most likely-a shot you as an intruder, you go sneaking up on him."

"I'm sorry," I whisper.

He calls out to Tolliver then, pressing the back of his hand against the boy's forehead. "Simon, buddy, we gotta go."

The doctor picks the boy up and Tolliver comes over, wrapping him in a military-looking surplus blanket.

"All right, let's get a move on," the doctor says. "Kid, we'll drop you off at the police station on the way."

"No," I plead. "No, please, I just want to go home."

He nods. "Okay, well, then, hurry. Come on."

We all walk out together, Tolliver carrying his son.

The doctor fires up the engine.

Tolliver holds his boy in his arms.

We drive fast to the hospital.

And I think about Teddy.

The fog closes in around us.

And we drive.

35.

THE BUS UP THE 101 from Mercy Hospital lumbers through the night. Up here, closer to the city, the fog has been blown clear and there is only the starless black above reflecting the toxic glow of the lights downtown.

There's only one other person on the bus, a young guy, probably just a little older than me, wearing big studio headphones and bobbing his head to whatever music he's listening to.

I sit at the very back of the bus with my body folded up, hugging my knees tightly and rocking slightly.

Simon Tolliver and the doctor were both super nice to me. They made me promise several times to go straight home. Tolliver even gave me a little money.

They put me on the bus and made sure I had everything I might need. Really, they were so sweet to me. I'm grateful.

And so goddamn sad.

Because it really, truly, is over now.

Teddy is gone. And I feel that in me just like I felt he was alive before. It's like somehow, inside of me, there is this knowledge that is real and deep and penetrating. Teddy is dead.

The voice whispers—that cool breeze again blowing through my mind, calming. It tells me that God's plan was not for me to save Teddy, but to accept his death and save myself. There was no way I could move on before. Now I can.

I can move on and finally be, fully and completely, with Eliza. That is God's will for me. It whispers in my ear and cools my brain even as I mourn Teddy and feel the tears burning my eyes.

I lay my head against the plastic of the bus window. My hands shake, and I cry and remember Teddy and remember how he used to be. I see him running on the beach that day. He's wading through the water, and it's blue and calm and perfect. I don't know how the hell that ocean could've swallowed him up. But it did. It swallowed him.

"*Eliza,*" the voice whispers.

Yes, Eliza. She is the missing piece.

I need to get back to her.

I need to be with her and I need to be with her now. I will tell her everything. I will make her understand.

Because it is over. And if I am going to survive this, I need to be with her. I am ready, and nothing is going to stop me.

The heat courses through my body, and there's sweat all down my neck and back. I get off the bus and transfer up Fulton to Divisadero and Hayes Street. It's a short walk up around the park to Eliza's.

I climb the stairs.

The crows begin to gather. Just on the edge of my vision, they swoop into position on the wires surrounding the house. They peck at their own dark feathers with their sharp, pointed beaks. Preening. Rolling their heads. Staring with their shiny black shark eyes.

I try the door and it swings open.

The crows caw at me, spreading their wings wide. They press in now, flying down onto the railing, settling on the concrete near my feet.

Dozens more take their places on the wires, the lawn, the trees. A number of them settle on a car parked in the driveway.

The car. Not Eliza's. Not her mother's.

A feeling like dread forms in my stomach and shoots up along my spine. "Eliza?" I call. There is no answer.

I push inside, scan the living room. The crows—they are here, too. Scattered across the carpet, perched on the walls of bookshelves.

There are more and more of them screeching into the room, swooping in from outside and upstairs.

I hear a shout.

It is Eliza.

I hear the voice again, whispering. *"The crows, they have her."*

I run, sprinting up to her bedroom. The birds cry, seemingly all at once.

I throw her door open.

Eliza is on her bed, and she is covered in them. She cries out, screams as they devour her.

"Stop!" I yell. "Stop! Get off of her!"

I grab their oily bodies. Throw them off her, pulling them apart, hitting them, strangling them, repeating all the while, "I'm here, Eliza. I'm here I'm here!"

I swing my fists and pound and tear and pull until I feel my hands slick with blood. I will tear them apart for touching her. I will destroy them.

"Miles! Jesus, what are you doing?" Eliza screams.

"Get off. Get off," I yell at the crows, punching and grabbing at them.

"Miles, stop!"

The crows swarm on me and I'm thrown back. I fall onto the hardwood floor and hit my head hard.

Eliza kneels in front of me. "Miles!" My eyes blur and water and I blink and blink again.

Eliza has a blanket wrapped around her body to cover herself. I turn to face the birds, to defend against another attack. But the crows are gone. Vanished.

On the floor beside me I see that kid—what's his name? From Preston's party. He's holding his bleeding mouth and nose. And he's naked.

"What is this?" I shake my head, trying to understand.

"Dude, Miles, this isn't what you think," the guy says, standing. I remember now—Kevin.

"Wait . . . what?"

I turn toward Eliza.

And I get it.

"Fuck," I say.

Then I drop to my knees and vomit. The hot liquid bursts out of my nose and throat.

"Miles!" Eliza screams. "Miles . . . Jesus."

The guy walks back over to the bed and starts putting his clothes on. He laughs then, telling us, "You're both fucking crazy." He gathers his shoes and socks in his arms and storms out the door.

I vomit again as he walks past.

"Fuck," I say.

Eliza comes over to try to help me, but I yell at her to leave me alone.

I get up off the floor, shaky, breathing heavily.

"I'm sorry," Eliza pleads with me, sitting back on the bed. "I'm sorry. I'm sorry."

"No!" I scream at the top of my lungs. "Fuck you. Fuck! You!"

I trip over myself and fall and then I get up again and go running down the stairs.

I want to scream and fight and tear myself apart now.

Outside the air is cold and still.

The crows are gone.

And so is everything else in my whole fucking world.

36.

IT IS DARK AND everyone is asleep by the time I get home.

I walk silently to my dad's office and then to the bathroom.

The knife I'm using was a wedding present given to my parents that has never actually been used—as far as I know. It's Japanese—large, almost like a butcher's knife. I had to take it from a fancy wooden box in the top drawer of the rolltop desk in my father's office.

I'm using the expensive knife because I know it will be sharp—much sharper than that dull-as-shit Ikea knife set we have in the kitchen.

I take the blade into the tub, wearing my sweat pants—because I totally don't want to be stark naked when they find me.

I sit cross-legged with my back pressed up against the mildewed tile.

The drops of water left over from whoever took a shower last are soaking into my pants, and the smell of soap and shampoo and whatever else is overpowering.

I breathe out long and slow.

The bathroom is small and cramped and bright and I would've preferred to light some candles or something, but I guess I have to make do with what I've got.

There aren't any pictures in here at all—only the mirror over the sink and a lot of toiletries and dried flowers and bath salts and my mother's pretty perfume bottles she never uses.

I decide to cut my right wrist first, holding the knife in my left, 'cause my right hand is much stronger. That way, once my right wrist is done, I'll still be able to use the hand to finish the job.

The voice is whispering softly, telling me that this is what I deserve. I have destroyed everything. This is all that is left.

"You are a parasite," it tells me. *"You aren't fit for survival. You are a burden on your family. You are a burden on humanity. You are sick, diseased. The world will be better off without you."*

It tells me what to do.

"Cut with the knife," it says. *"Start with the right one."*

And so I do as it says. I take the knife in my left hand and cut it into my right wrist. I try to do it fast, without even thinking about it. I draw the knife quickly and deeply straight across the veins. It stings like a motherfucker. That's what I can say. It stings and burns and it fucking hurts.

It hurts so much that I drop the knife. I'm struggling for breath like I've just jumped into the freezing cold ocean. A thousand needles cover me and the blood comes—deep purplish, crimson, black.

Somehow I do manage to grab the knife with my right hand, though, just like I'd planned. Gritting my teeth, I draw it quickly, albeit less deeply, across the other wrist.

This time I vomit. I flop onto my side and throw up into the shower drain. I choke and cough and wretch as the vomit forces itself up and out of my throat. I'm covered in blood and puke and I feel myself quickly passing out.

The only thing left to do now is call 911 to make sure the EMTs find me before my parents do—or, God forbid, Jane. To scar her like that would be worse than anything. I can't let that happen—no matter what.

So I swing my body back around to where I put my phone. Luckily, 911 is pretty easy to dial, even with both wrists sliced open—but I guess that's probably the point.

My twitching fingers find the numbers and I wait, fighting to stay conscious.

Click.

"Nine-one-one Emergency, how can I help you?"

My breathing comes fast and shallow, so I can barely get the words to come out of me.

"Th- . . . th- . . . there's been a . . . No, I . . . I killed myself."

Pause.

"What? I'm sorry, sir, what? Can you repeat that?"

More breathing.

"I . . . I . . . I said I killed myself. 1717 Clement Street."

"You killed yourself?"

I close my eyes.

"Th- . . . the back bathroom."

"What? Hello, sir, are you there? Please stay on the line with me, sir."

I feel tired suddenly—so deeply fucking tired.

The curtain falls.

There is only darkness.

PART THREE

37.

IT TAKES ME A few moments to realize what's happened and where I am.

The room is bright and blinding. I'm being choked by something so I can't talk, but I need to. I need help right away. There is this giant plastic tube down my throat and my eyes are watering and I keep on gagging as I call out, "Ahhhhh! Ahhhhhh!"

And then a nurse is there standing in front of me, cocking her head to one side as my eyes go wide and I jerk my body back and forth, still gagging, and begging her to get this thing out of my throat.

"Aughhh! Aughhhh!"

She leaves then, if you can believe that. She leaves, and so I start flailing and making as much noise as I can to get them to pay attention to me and get this thing out of me.

I'm not sure how long that lasts, but finally two nurses come in—and one, this large drag-queen-looking guy, says to me, "Just hold on, sugah." And he holds on to me while the other nurse pulls the tube out of my stomach and out of my throat and I gag and breathe and gasp for more and more breath.

"Well, you awake now, honey. Good. The doctor will be here shortly."

And then the other nurse starts messing around with one of the IV drips I have going and shoots in what I imagine must be a bunch of morphine, 'cause I start to fade out again pretty quick after that.

"You sleep," the nice drag-queeny one says. "The doctor will come."

I nod my head—trying to say thank you, but my throat's burning too bad.

"Shhh, shhh, don't talk."

My eyes close again.

And that's when . . . suddenly . . . I remember.

I failed.

Again.

38.

WAKING A SECOND TIME, I sit up all at once out of the deepest blackness. There is someone there, next to me, whispering in my ear.

"Get out. Get out of here."

The brightness floods in and I blink my eyes and call out, "Who's there?"

The voice speaks from some hidden place inside me.

"Get out of here. Get the fuck out of here."

My breath comes in gasps—my throat is dry and pained and raspy.

I grab at the needles all stuck in my arms and pull them free, along with the tape that held them fastened.

"Get out! Get out!"

There is a plastic curtain around my bed that I take hold of to try to hoist myself up, but it tears away from the metal frame and I find myself sprawled out on the cold, chemical-smelling linoleum, the curtain all tangled around me.

"Get out! Get out!"

I start to crawl, but something is stopping me—something at my waist. I reach down and feel what is there, burning and tugging at the place between my legs.

"Get out!"

"I will get out," I say aloud. "I will get out."

There is a piercing noise like an alarm going off loud in my ears.

"Help me!" I yell. "Help me! Get this out of me."

But the voice has abandoned me suddenly.

"Hello? Hello? Help me. Hello?"

There is nothing but the alarm screaming. It screams like a siren.

I hold my palms up against my ears.

And then someone else is there, holding me under my arms.

"Jésus Cristo, kid."

My head thrashes wildly.

I feel myself being lifted up.

"Hold him. Hold him."

The burning between my legs intensifies.

"Get off of me!" I yell. "What the fuck!"

There is a great pressure on my chest and then something sharp cutting into my side.

"Get him down. Hold him."

The alarm stops screaming at me then, but the pain in my side just keeps getting worse and fucking worse.

I'm having trouble breathing.

"Your ribs are broken," says a voice, "from the CPR. Lie still."

I do as I'm told.

I lie, blinking my eyes and trying to see.

"I'm sorry," I say. "Someone was here. Someone was making me leave."

And then there is a loud sobbing noise next to me, and I turn and finally recognize something: my mother.

She is hunched over, crying, her shoulders heaving, and at the same time shouting, "He needs his medication! Please! I told you! He needs his medication!"

She is very pale-looking, and her gray hair is knotted on top of her head.

"Goddamnit," I say hoarsely. This is exactly what I didn't want.

I feel the almost weightlessness of my mom's frail hand on my shoulder.

"Hush, now, Mie. Hush, baby." And then louder, to the nurses, or whoever else is there, "He needs his medication."

"Please," I whisper.

There is the prick of a needle in the crook of my arm and then a warmth flooding me.

"Am I peeing?" I ask.

And then it's all black again.

39.

MY MOTHER IS THERE and my father, too, both staring at me intently as my eyes try to focus.

"That's better now, isn't it?" my mom asks me—and I have to admit that it is.

I feel calm and clear for the first time.

I know fully where I am.

I mean, I'm in the hospital.

There are needles stuck in me connected to fluid drips and a catheter up in between my legs—which must've been what remained attached to me when I tried to run away. There are machines monitoring my heart rate and my blood pressure. There are thick bandages wrapped around both arms. Fuck, man, they've stitched me up and put me back together again. And they must've gotten me on the right meds now, too, because I'm not acting all psycho.

"Mom?"

She smiles. "Yes, yes. I'm here."

I smile back, suddenly aware of how parched I am. My tongue is thick and swollen.

"W- . . . water? Is there water?"

My mom turns, and I can see that my dad is standing there behind her. My request triggers a chain reaction of people looking over their shoulders. My mom, my dad, the doctor, a male nurse. Actually, it stops at him. He goes off, returning a second later with a plastic cup in his hand.

"Here you go," he says, his voice deep and startling.

He helps me to sit up and take the cup with my right hand. The wrists on both sides are still sore as fucking hell.

I gulp down the water.

"Th- . . . thank you," I manage to say.

He bows his head, and then the doctor comes over and puts a callused hand on my forehead. He speaks very gently.

"You are still running a slight fever. But the worst of it should be over now."

"Thank you," I say again.

He nods, adjusting the stethoscope hanging around his neck. "My name is Dr. Fliederer, Miles. I was the doctor on call the night you . . ." He pauses. "Came in here."

His eyes are so transparent and blue and kind, I can't help but look away.

"Oh," I say dumbly.

"And now," he continues, audibly tapping his foot on the

linoleum, "well, I've been working with your parents on your continuing care plan."

My dad steps forward at that moment. His skin is gray and ashen-looking.

"Hey, buddy," he says, putting his hand up.

I smile. "Hey, Dad."

My voice cracks. I can see his eyes are red and swollen from crying, and I think maybe I might cry then, too. I mean, he looks so helpless standing there, so awkward and unsure.

"We just want to do what's best for you," he says, shifting his weight from one foot to the other.

"That's right," my mom says, walking up between my dad and the doctor, moving some hair back from my eyes. She leans forward and kisses my cheek. I try to smell the smell of her, but hospital disinfectant and plastic obscures everything else. "We just want what's best for you," she repeats.

It's fucking cold in here, so I'm shivering. The shivering runs all the way through me. I don't know, maybe it's the fever. All I know is that I want to sleep again so badly it hurts.

My joints crack and I go on shivering.

"It . . . ," I start. "I m-mean, it's s-so cold. Could we . . . Is there a heater?"

My parents both look at the doctor, who, again, looks at the nurse. "Could you bring Miles another couple blankets?" he asks him. And then to me: "I'm sorry, Miles. It's a hospital."

I shiver. "Oh . . . okay."

"What you need is some more rest," he says.

I nod.

"Yes, good," he continues on. "That's good. We just wanted to talk to you very briefly, your mother and father and I, about your aftercare plan. And I believe we've found the best possible solution for your situation."

I manage to laugh a little. "A brain transplant?"

The doctor smiles, still looking very kind. "No, I'm afraid not. But we have gotten you on a new medication. It's called Clozaril and it's proven to be somewhat of a miracle drug with severe schizophrenic patients. So that's something to be hopeful about. And we are going to transfer you to our psych ward here at the hospital and keep you on a seventy-two-hour hold where you'll be seen by our specialist, Dr. Dubonis. Do you understand all that?"

My attention shifts over to my mom then, who has started crying, however silently. She holds my stare and smiles through her tears.

"A psych ward?" I ask, my teeth starting to chatter.

My mom's eyes remain fixed on mine. She nods slowly. "It's just for a few days."

"Christ, fuck," I say, the tears coming now. "I'm sorry. Please, can't I just come home?"

The doctor clears his throat again. "No, Miles. You need to get well. I'm afraid there's no choice."

My mom puts a hand on my forehead as I start to cry. "Hush, now, hush."

She has just the saddest, sweetest smile. My dad, too, really.

I lie back down on the bed and let my eyes start to close.

"E- . . . Eliza?" I say, half sleeping already. "Does Eliza know?"

The sound of the overhead fluorescent lighting is loud, crackling through the silence.

"Don't worry," my dad finally whispers. "That's all behind you now."

He puts a hand gently on my forehead and tells me again not to worry.

I turn, shivering, onto my side.

I pull the blanket up over my head.

I sleep, but do not dream.

I know now I will never dream again.

Because in my life, there are no dreams left.

PART FOUR

40.

THE GROUP ROOM IS pretty much the same as my room in the ward, but with a couple motivational posters on the wall and, instead of beds, a circle of plastic orange chairs.

Dr. Dubonis, the primary care physician on the unit, sits with his back facing the two caged windows. He is very thin and sickly-looking, with pale yellow pockmarked skin and a scruffy, graying beard. His hands are large and appear to be covered in some kind of sores or blisters that he keeps picking at with his long thumbnail. He is fidgety and jerks around a lot and seems like he should be a patient here, not the doctor in charge of us all. But the little pin on his uniform does read *Henry Dubonis, MD,* so I guess he must be legit. Plus everyone else seems to be looking at him like he's in charge.

There is a whiteboard on wheels behind him with the acronym

H.A.L.T. written across it with a nearly dried-up red marker. It's an acronym I'm familiar with.

H.A.L.T.: Hungry. Angry. Lonely. Tired.

Meaning, in order not to go crazy, you're never supposed to let yourself get too hungry, angry, lonely, or tired.

It's actually pretty good advice, I'd say. Even if it does happen to be in the lexicon of pretty much every goddamn therapist ever.

At least, that's been my experience.

But, anyway, H.A.L.T. Sure, it makes sense.

Dr. Dubonis explains the whole thing a couple times while everyone takes their seats, and then he goes on and turns his attention to me—which makes me cross my arms and legs and try to make myself just as small as I can.

"Well, now, as I'm sure you've all noticed, we have a new patient today, and I thought, before we get started—"

A girl just to the left of me stamps her foot and leans forward, putting her elbows on her knees, shouting, "Nah, fuck, man, let's start. Let's get this fucking over with."

She's Japanese, I think—with an accent and everything. Punk-looking with short-cut hair dyed different shades of red and all these tattoos and white scars up and down her arms. She wears a ripped-up tank top and loose-fitting pajama bottoms. Actually, pretty much everyone is wearing pajamas. Even the tranny with his/her makeup done and a long black wig and press-on nails is wearing pajamas and fuzzy little slippers. Well, not that little. His/her feet are at least a size twelve or thirteen.

"Ha, where you got to go, Yuka?" he/she calls out. "You ain't goin' nowhere. Shit."

A couple of the other patients laugh, but the Japanese girl, Yuka, just kind of scrunches her face all up and then kicks the ground again.

"Fuck you, Sweet Pea," she yells. "I got places, man, fuck you."

There's some more laughter, and then Dr. Dubonis clears his throat a couple times.

"Sweet Pea, Yuka, please," he says, but not angrily. "We have a new patient, and—"

This real weird-looking psycho kid cuts in, "You said that already." His head is shaved, with cuts all over it.

"Yes, well," Dr. Dubonis continues, picking more at his scabby hands. "Nonetheless, this is Miles Cole. He's going to be with us for a while."

I shift around in the hard plastic seat, feeling all the eyes turned on me—eyes like the crows' eyes, black and vacant and darting.

Dr. Dubonis leans forward, talking to me gently.

"Would you like to tell us about yourself, Miles? Can you tell the group why you're here?"

"Uh . . . yeah . . . I'm . . . uh, Miles."

That's my brilliant introduction.

"Fucking said that already," the psycho kid with all the cuts says, rolling his eyes.

A shy, sweet-looking kid chews on his dirty fingernails and stutters, "L-l-let him t-talk."

Dr. Dubonis smiles, encouraging. "Yes, thank you, Max." And then to me, "Go ahead, Miles."

I nod. "Well . . . uh . . . I tried to kill myself," I say. "But I didn't."

There's some laughter.

One girl, small, with mousy brown hair, tells me, "Congratulations," all sarcastic-like.

"Well, would you like to share your diagnosis with us?" the doctor asks me, not letting up.

I shrink back into my chair a little more. "Sch- . . . schizophrenia."

A few of the patients clap.

Dr. Dubonis smiles. "Good. Very good. Should we go around, then, and introduce ourselves and tell Miles why we're here?"

Yuka stands up suddenly, knocking her chair over and then kicking it when it's down.

"Fuck this!" she shouts.

Dr. Dubonis is up then, too, but like he's aware of keeping his distance from her.

"Do you not feel like joining us today, Yuka?"

She flips him off and yells at all of us, "Fuck you, fucking assholes."

She stomps toward the door, but then almost instantly there are two men in white uniforms grabbing hold of her as she screams and kicks and flails her arms.

"Get off me! Get the fuck off of me."

"You'll come back to group when you've calmed down a little bit, okay?" the doctor says.

And then the two men carry her off, screaming all the way down the hall about how we could all go fuck ourselves.

Dr. Dubonis goes and sits back down and smiles, and no one else seems to care that someone was dragged from the room against her will—though, I figure, maybe they're just used to it.

"Okay, sorry all," the doctor says cheerfully. "Where were we?"

As if in response, this one boy, who'd been sitting very quietly, suddenly jerks up and makes this terrible screaming noise super loud that startles the shit out of me. Well, actually, no, it's not a scream exactly. It's like the sound is forcing itself out of his body. He trembles and shakes and then the vocalizations come pouring out of his mouth, like, "Awwwaaaaahh . . . awwahhh!"

It happens two or three times in a row.

"Jesus Christ," this super overweight goth-looking girl says, rolling her eyes. "This is such a waste of time."

The boy does his weird vocalization thing again. "Awwaah-haaa!"

The tranny, Sweet Pea, crosses and uncrosses his/her legs. "Ain't that the truth?"

The boy screams out.

He keeps on screaming.

He screams for all of us.

41.

LOOKING OUT THE SMALL, caged window above my bed, I can see crows gathering in the treetops, silhouetted by the perpetually gray sky.

The sun is obscured by the heavy mist coming in from the ocean. There is only the gray and the tops of the trees and the crows circling there and the cage around my window.

My window in my room.

My room in the goddamn psych ward.

I stand on the frame of my bed, watching as the crows dive and circle.

I think about Eliza.

I try not to think about Eliza.

I feel sick in my stomach.

I feel like I could cry, maybe.

The door opens behind me.

I turn around.

It's that kid, Max, from the group earlier.

He must be my roommate.

He's real thin and hollowed-out-looking—his hair all choppy, like he cut it himself.

He keeps his eyes on the ground when he talks and has a super bad stutter. I figure he must be maybe a year or two older than I am, but definitely not more.

"Oh . . . uh . . . y-y-you're in here, then?"

"Yeah, is that okay?"

He walks over to the closet where he takes a wool cardigan off one of the wooden hangers. "Uh . . . uh . . . of course." He sits down on his bed, clearing away some of the magazines. "H-h-have you b-b-been shown where everything is yet?"

Really, he seems nice enough, so I smile and sit down on my own bed. "Yeah, thanks, I think so."

We sit quietly for a few moments.

He crosses his legs, and so I cross mine, too.

"So, uh," I say, "what are you doing here? You don't seem crazy like the rest of them."

He smiles shyly. "I c-can't function in the r-real world."

"Yeah. Me neither."

42.

THE STAFF ROOM IS tiny and cramped and overcrowded with filing cabinets and stacks of patients' charts and VHS tapes. The door is half open, and I stand there for a few seconds waiting to be noticed by the giant woman looking at a *People* magazine or the paunchy white guy with greasy hair thinning on his head. The name tag pinned to his chest reads *Carl.* The one pinned to the woman's chest reads *Edna.*

Edna and Carl.

I knock gently on the door. Edna looks up and squints at me through her thick horn-rimmed glasses. She doesn't appear to be too thrilled about me having interrupted her.

"Yes?" she asks. "Can we help you with something?"

Her skin is creased and leathery like an old, worn-out suitcase. Her eyes are black fading to gray around the edges. She's wearing a lot of lipstick and has painted-on eyebrows.

She taps her white orthopedic hospital shoes like she wants me to get to the point.

"Sorry," I say, my voice faltering. "I just . . . uh . . . Someone paged me?"

She takes off her glasses, cleaning them on the white thermal undershirt she's wearing beneath her blue scrubs. She turns to look over behind her at this big whiteboard hanging on the wall. There's a list written on it of a bunch of patients' names cross-referenced with time slots where different appointments have been filled in. I see my own name, since it's at the top of the list, and then next to it, in red marker: *Doctor S. Frankel.*

"You see that?" Edna asks me.

"Yeah."

"So you're gonna have to hurry, okay? You've got your meeting with your doctor."

"Dr. Frankel?"

"Yes, he's your private psychiatrist, isn't he?"

"Yeah, but . . . what's he doing here?"

She lets her shoulders rise and fall. "Guess your parents must've set it up."

I nod.

"So you better get down there, huh?" she continues, kind of sarcastic-sounding. "You know the way?"

I tell her I don't, and so, begrudgingly, she pushes up from her chair with considerable effort and tells me to follow her.

She walks out the door, and so I do, too.

43.

DR. FRANKEL IS SITTING in a hard plastic chair in one of the visiting rooms. He looks the same as ever, wearing that stupid tracksuit, with his short, stubby legs dangling inches off the ground.

Still, I have to admit, there's something kind of comforting about seeing him again.

"Miles, my boy," he says. "I'm so sorry about all this."

He gestures to the seat across from him and so I sit down, crossing my legs and arms.

"It was my fault," I tell him. "I stopped taking my medication. I flushed it. All of it."

He reaches out his hand as though to comfort me, but then stops himself—I guess remembering some doctor/patient bullshit or whatever.

"It wasn't your fault, my boy. It was nobody's fault. Can you tell me what happened?"

I nod. "Yeah, I guess so."

"Just take your time. It's all going to be all right."

I nod some more, staring down at my shoes, chewing at the inside of my cheek. But as soon as I start talking, it all comes pouring out of me, everything: about the crows, the voice, Eliza, Teddy being dead.

"Teddy." Dr. Frankel stops me, holding his hand up. "You've talked about him before, haven't you?"

"Yeah, of course."

He clears his throat. "Yes, but who is this Teddy?"

"What do you mean? Teddy. My brother—the one I thought was kidnapped."

He squints at me. "I . . . I didn't realize you thought he was your brother."

It's my turn to ask him now, "What do you mean, *thought* he was my brother? He is my brother. He's dead, though. I've come to accept that."

Dr. Frankel stares at me for a moment as though turning something around in his brain.

"Miles . . . you don't have a brother. You have a sister."

I clench my fist tightly.

"Of course I do. . . . Or did. Teddy Bryant Cole. He went missing the same day I had my first episode at Ocean Beach. I thought he'd been kidnapped. I've been trying to track him down. But now I know he must've drowned. Everyone tried to tell me. I wouldn't listen."

"Teddy Bryant?"

"Teddy Bryant Cole—yeah. My brother."

He breathes in through his nose. "Miles . . . I'm sorry, but you have no brother. I don't know how to make you understand. But you have no brother. This is . . . It must be a delusion brought on by your illness."

I jump to my feet then, knocking over the chair behind me in the process. There's this heat burning through me, and I feel my heart pounding in my head and I can't even hear as I yell, "You don't know what you're talking about. What the hell are you talking about? Jesus Christ, you're all fucking crazy. You're fucking crazy."

He says something to me I can't hear, but I don't fucking care. I scream, "Fuck you—just leave me alone," and I storm out. There is a sickness in my stomach and I feel my head spin and a sweat breaks out all over my body.

This is crazy. This whole thing. The world spins around and around, and then my eyes roll back and it all goes black.

44.

THROUGH THE BLUR of too-bright light I see Dr. Dubonis looking down at me. He smiles then and helps me sit up, and I see that I'm lying on the couch in his office. Dr. Frankel is there looking through a stack of papers behind Dr. Dubonis's rolltop desk in the corner.

"Here, Miles, drink this," Dr. Dubonis tells me, handing over a paper cup filled with water and what I think is some Emergen-C, electrolyte whatever.

I do as I'm told and then I try to stand up, but it's like my legs don't work.

"Just hold on," Dr. Dubonis says, putting a hand on my shoulder. "Dr. Frankel and I . . . We want to talk to you about something."

My jaw clicks back and forth. "About my brother?"

237

"Miles," Dr. Frankel says, "I know this is hard for you, but . . . listen. That name, Teddy Bryant, I knew it sounded familiar."

"Yeah, duh, my brother."

"Miles, please, just listen," Dr. Dubonis tells me.

Dr. Frankel leans forward, handing me the stack of papers. "Teddy Bryant," Dr. Frankel says, "is the name of a child who *did* disappear. You're not wrong about that. But . . . he's not your brother."

I look down at the papers in my hands, but the words are all blurred out. There is a picture of Teddy, though. That's certain.

"This is him," I say. "This is Teddy."

"Yes, Miles. Yes. It is Teddy. But, look, Dr. Dubonis printed these just now. They're from the *Chronicle* website. Can you see what it says there?"

I squint and try to make out the words. "It's an article about Teddy . . . from when he disappeared."

"Yes, but look, Miles. It's Teddy Bryant. Of the Bryant family.

"Teddy Bryant," he continues, "is the son of Bruce and Lorraine Bryant. He has a sister, Sophie Bryant. He was seven years old when, two years ago, he disappeared from Ocean Beach. According to your file, it was exactly one week after you had your first psychotic episode at that same beach. You were probably still in the hospital and still recuperating from your attack when the story of the Bryant boy's disappearance was all over the news. After your episode, you were experiencing intense guilt and feelings of shame. You blamed yourself. And you thought your family blamed you. Somehow the news of Teddy Bryant's disappearance got all mixed together with your guilt for what you believed you were doing to your parents. The Bryant boy became the physical manifestation of your guilt. Your subconscious needed to assign your guilt to something solid and concrete—like a missing brother."

I listen, flipping through the article in front of me. I read the names Bruce and Lorraine Bryant. I read the date. I read the description of the incident.

Dr. Frankel leans forward and smiles at me, his eyes flashing kindness and warmth. My hands begin to shake as I turn the pages over and over.

"You mean . . . ," I start, my voice shaking just as badly as my hands. "You mean, all this time? For two years I've been blaming myself . . . I've been . . . trying to . . . You mean . . . it was all a . . ."

Could this possibly be true?

Tears burn in my eyes.

"Part of your disease," he says gently.

My mind flashes back to the police department. *Teddy Bryant,* the lady at the front desk said. But I added the Cole. *Teddy Bryant Cole,* I'd said, but she was already on the phone, trying to get that detective for me.

The file I stole. The date that was wrong.

Except it wasn't wrong. I was wrong—or just fucking crazy.

Jane and my mom and dad—I kept apologizing to them for what happened. I thought they knew I was talking about Teddy. But they must've thought I was talking about my sickness.

My mom's office. The house. No pictures anywhere. No pictures because there never was a Teddy Bryant Cole.

There was only me.

I nod and shiver.

"Jesus, fuck, I'm crazy. I'm fucking crazy."

Dr. Frankel leans forward and this time puts a hand gently on my back. "You're not crazy. You're sick."

"Sick and fucking crazy."

"But this means you're free now, can't you see that? You never hurt anyone. You're not responsible. You can stop punishing yourself. You can let yourself live again."

I feel the barely there pressure of his hand on my back and I breathe and I close my eyes.

The son of a bitch is right.

If there's no Teddy Cole, then I can't very well go on blaming myself for his disappearance.

If there's no Teddy Cole, then I did nothing wrong.

If there's no Teddy Cole . . .

There *is* no Teddy Cole.

For two years he was all I could think about, all I would *let* myself think about.

Without that, what do I have?

Without that, who am I?

45.

CLOZARIL, MAN, I HATE sounding like a goddamn adver-
tisement, but it does seem to be working. The crows are gone,
Teddy is gone, the voice of God or the universe or whatever is
gone, even my obsession with Eliza seems pretty well gone.

From what both doctors say, I'd come to hate myself because
of my disease. And so I was always, like, desperately trying as
hard as I could to run away from the fact that I was mentally ill.

But in here, they're trying to teach me how to accept my
illness and learn how to love myself (as fucking lame as that
sounds) in spite of it. They keep telling me it's not my fault. And
I know it's not my fault, but I guess I don't always feel that way.
So they're trying to get me to know it, like, for real inside of me.

It's all easier said than done, but I'm working on it. And it
is getting easier. If anything, being with the people here, I've al-

most started to feel a little proud of my illness. Well, not proud of it exactly, but proud that I'm facing it and finally learning how to live.

The people I've met in here, they are some strong mother-fuckers. Sweet Pea, Yuka, my roommate, Max. They've all been through more shit than anyone I've ever met before. And they are good people. Emotionally disturbed, sure, but good people nonetheless.

Of all the kids in here, it's really that poor Steven who's the hardest to figure out. Those vocalization things seem to get worse whenever he's in group or talking about any kind of emotional anything. When he's just hanging out watching TV or something they go away. It's totally weird. But he's super nice—gentle and sweet.

He sits cross-legged in the group and rocks back and forth.

There's a podium set up, and this young, very pretty woman, probably around thirty-five, is going on and on about how great her life is now even though she's a schizo, like us.

The woman said her name at the beginning of her share, but I can't remember it now. She's wearing a collared shirt and jeans and has really long, slender fingers that keep tapping on the podium as she talks.

To tell you the truth, most of what she's said so far has kind of just blended together into one generic self-help amalga-mation. But then . . . slowly . . . a little bit at a time . . . I start focusing more on what it is she's actually saying, and it's crazy how similar her delusions were to mine. Not about Teddy or making up some person that doesn't even exist, but about God talking to her like I thought he was talking to me. About that power coming into her life the same way it did into mine.

She takes a drink of water from the bottle on the podium. "And I really believed it. I thought God was telling me things. To the point that God was telling me I should jump off the Golden Gate Bridge so I could prove to the world that I was an angel."

She goes on to tell the story of how she tried to jump off the Golden Gate Bridge, but was stopped by a man riding across on his bike. Then she tells us how she got into treatment and got on medication, and the rest is pretty typical, I guess.

But that stuff about God talking to her and all that, I keep on playing it over and over in my mind.

The woman finishes her talk and a few people clap.

Wanika, this girl around my age who's super nice—and super beautiful—gives me a look with her eyes wide and we go out to the balcony together to smoke.

"Jesus Christ," I say, leaning out into the gray, looking down on the back loading dock.

"Yeah," she says. "Another fun-filled day in the psych ward."

I drag on my cigarette and ash over the railing. "You're leaving tomorrow?" I ask, even though I know the answer to my own question.

She nods.

"You think you're ready?"

"Yes, I think I'm ready. What about you? You're leaving tomorrow, too, right?"

"Yeah."

I pause and think and pick at my thumbnail.

"How . . . how do you deal with knowing that so much of what you thought was real . . . totally wasn't? Like that woman thinking God was talking to her and everything."

She smiles. "Or like you and your fake dead brother?"

"Exactly. I just don't know how we're gonna do this. Or how I will, anyway . . ."

"Yeah, man, I get it. The other day I had my mom bring in one of my old notebooks. I wanted to see what the hell I'd been writing all that time. You know what it was? Pages and pages of tiny little symbols. No words. Scribbles. Fucking crazy."

I sit down next to Wanika and cross my legs and tell her, "I didn't just have an imaginary brother. All that God stuff she was talking about, I'm serious, I felt the same way—like God was talking to me."

She laughs and her eyes turn brighter green and her teeth flash white and I think, for the fifty-billionth time, how goddamn beautiful she is—and how that shouldn't matter at all.

"That's nothing," she says. "I think we've all had God talking to us at one point or another."

"Really?"

"Really."

The sliding glass door opens then, and that creepy Carl comes lurking out. "You know you aren't allowed to be out here without supervision?"

Wanika narrows her eyes at him. "We'll come inside in a minute."

"No, you'll come inside now." He stands watching us from the doorway.

Wanika puts her hand on my shoulder. "Look," she says, "you can do this. I don't wanna see you turn into one of these people who end up stuck in institutions their whole life. Like that roommate of yours. He's been in and out of psych wards for over three years. He could leave if he wanted to; he's just too scared."

"Yeah, I know. But I want to go home. I want to be with my friends and family again."

She turns to look at me. "What about that girl, huh?"

I stub my cigarette out in the ashtray. "Eliza? No. I don't want to see her."

"Good. Because she sounds like a bitch to me."

I shake my head. "She's not a bitch."

"Trust me, man, I can be a bitch—so I know what I'm saying when I say that *she* is a bitch."

I laugh with her. She is such a strong, beautiful girl. Dr. Frankel is right. I need friends right now. And I think maybe Wanika is my friend.

"Look," she continues, "you're sick, I'm sick. You made up

an imaginary brother; I stalked my anthropology teacher. But
you're a good fucking person. And I'm a good fucking person.
The only reason we did that shit was because we were sick. But
so what? We're fucking sick and we take medication. What's
the big deal? Would you be blaming yourself if you had fucking
cancer or some shit?"

I laugh. "Probably."

"Well, that's because you're a nice person. But you gotta
stop it. Stop being so nice."

"Okay," I say. "I'll try."

She stands up straight, and I stand up, too.

"Thank you," I tell her. "You're sweet to me."

"We're both gettin' out of here tomorrow, man. We gotta
stick together."

"We will."

Carl yells at us again to come inside.

Wanika takes my hand in hers.

And we go in together.

46.

TODAY I LEAVE the psych ward.

I'm fucking scared, but I'm ready.

The only thing is, in order to agree to let me leave, Dr. Frankel and Dr. Dubonis want me to have a meeting with my parents to finally talk about Teddy and what that means going forward. Because as it is now, I still haven't told them anything about what happened.

I guess it makes sense. Keeping our disease a secret—and hiding our symptoms—is part of what makes recovery from this fucking thing so goddamn hard. That's what they say here, anyway. I've got to learn how to open up about my illness. Like those crows I was seeing all the time; I should've talked about them with someone—Dr. Frankel, at least.

If there's a silver goddamn lining to all this, it's that I'm learning to manage my illness. It doesn't get any fucking better than that.

But, still, that's not so bad. Not really.

So I make my bed like I'm supposed to every day.

I make my bed, and Max makes his bed and he says to me, "Y-your parents coming today?"

"Uh-huh." I nod.

He keeps on scratching behind his ear and does a little head twitch thing. "G-good luck."

I reach out my hand. He shakes it nervously.

"Thanks, man."

Both Dr. Frankel and Dr. Dubonis are already in the group room, sitting and talking with my mom and dad.

My parents have been here several times before, obviously, but it's actually the first time we're all meeting together, with both of my doctors.

It's a gray day. The cold light streams dully across the polished linoleum tile floor. Artwork is hung around the room—including one of my own drawings done with colored pencils and charcoal, faces coming out of faces, crows circling a young boy crouched on the sand.

I walk into the room, and my mom and dad both get up and they hug me, and my dad says, "We're proud of you," and my mom says, "Hey."

She looks the same in many ways—pale, weathered, and exhausted. I wish she could change like I've changed in here.

Because I really have started to believe since being here that it's possible for me to live a good, normal life on medication. That's the biggest fucking gift they could've given me. And they have given it to me. I have hope. And it seems totally founded. We've had so many guest speakers come in to share with us about how great their lives are now that they're stabilized on medication.

And this new drug does seem to be pretty awesome.

So far, at least, I haven't had any hallucinations or heard any voices or anything. It *is* kind of a miracle, like Dr. Fliederer said to me that first day.

Not that I won't have relapses, as they call them, but as long as I'm honest about it, they can adjust my meds and I should be okay.

I guess that's the main fucking point. I will be okay.

I believe that now.

And I tell it to my mom and dad.

"I'm gonna be okay."

My dad smiles and puts his hand on my shoulder. He's shaved his beard and is wearing a button-down shirt.

"We do want you to come home," my mom says. "And we love you very much. But we're worried. At least in here, we know you're safe and taken care of. Coming home, we can't have you disappearing like you do, or going off and staying with some girl—like that Eliza."

I grind my teeth together. "Mom, I'm not seeing her anymore. I don't want to see anyone like that. I'm just gonna focus on myself and my recovery."

Dr. Frankel jumps in then to help me out, saying, "The way I understand it, Mrs. Cole, is that part of Miles's obsessive behavior with Eliza was due to the fact that he was simply on the wrong medication."

"That's right," Dr. Dubonis adds, looking at his clipboard as though reading something. "Miles appears to have been in a semi-psychotic, not properly medicated state for the entire two-year period following his first incident."

I'm looking at the mud dried on my shoes as my dad says, "Wait, I'm sorry. What do you mean exactly?"

Dr. Frankel turns and prompts me, though I still don't look up. "Do you want to tell him, Miles?"

I breathe in and out.

I kick the ground and grit my teeth and fidget with my hands.

I tell the story.

I tell them about Teddy and Dotty Peterson and Simon Tolliver.

By the end of the whole thing my mom and dad are both crying—my dad massaging my shoulder, my mom covering her face with her hands.

"Miles, we had no idea," my dad says. "Why didn't you tell us?"

"Well . . . because I thought it was all my fault. I wanted to protect you and Mom from having to think about it."

"But that is exactly the point," Dr. Dubonis says, clearing his throat as always. "We need to get an open dialogue going among the three of you. We need to make sure Miles is comfortable expressing any fears or doubts he might have. If he's feeling shaky—even just the littlest bit—it's imperative that he can come share that with you."

"Of course," my dad says. "That's what we want. That's what we've always wanted."

"And Miles knows that," Dr. Frankel adds. "We just wanted to bring it up so we're all starting on the same page."

My mom wipes her tears away and sits up straighter and pushes her hair back.

"But . . . do you think he's ready?" she asks, then turns to me. "Do you really think you're ready?"

I lean forward and can see the blue of her eyes bright against the red burning there. The tears well up and spill over again.

"Mom," I whisper hoarsely. "Mom. I'm sorry. I'm sorry, it's okay."

She looks up at me then, her face contorted, her eyes narrowed. "*Don't!* Don't say you're sorry, Miles. Please. Please don't say you're sorry."

She keeps on crying, and Dr. Frankel goes to get a box of tissues off the arts and crafts table.

"What's upsetting you so much right now?" he asks her, handing over a few tissues to my mom.

"I . . . I . . . I . . . ," she starts, blowing her nose. "I just feel so . . . so terrible that my . . . my son . . ." She turns to me.

"That I made you feel so guilty, that you had to invent this . . . this character. You always say you're sorry. But, Mie, *I'm* sorry."

She cries more, and I get up and say, "Mom, come on. It's okay. It's not your fault."

"That's right," says Dr. Dubonis. "It's not anyone's fault."

I hug my mom to me then, and she hugs me back, and I feel her frail body and smell the familiar smell of her.

"No more apologizing," my mom says.

"Yeah, well, you either," I tell her.

My dad stands up then, too, and rubs my back.

"If you can just stay honest with one another," Dr. Dubonis says, "then you shouldn't have any problems."

"But we're here if you need us," Dr. Frankel adds. "And Miles will have meetings with me twice a week."

"I know you're ready," my mom says to me, straightening my shirt. "I can see you are."

She hugs me again.

We all sit back down.

We finish the meeting.

We are all together.

And I am going home.

And everything is all right.

47.

THE MORNING AFTER I got home I wake up to the smell of bacon and cooked butter. Away from the psych ward the gray is gone and sunlight, warm and bright, fills the room.

It feels so safe and comforting being back in my own bed—not on a plastic mattress with rubber sheets and a thin, barely there blanket. I want to lie here forever—wrapped in the plush comforter, looking out on the world through my window, the telephone wires stretched across the skyline, with no crows looking back at me.

My hallucinations are gone. My head is clear. And I want to lie here, but breakfast smells too good, so I get up and pee and then wander into the kitchen.

"Milesy!" Jane calls, accentuating every syllable.

"Janey!" I say.

She walks over to me and gives me a hug, and I hug her, and even though I did see her last night, waking up and being with her today makes me feel like I'm really home—and that is good.

"Pancakes and bacon," she tells me. "Dad made pancakes and bacon."

"That's right," my dad hollers from the table. "Coffee, too."

"And orange juice," my mom says, startling me a little since she usually never eats breakfast with us at all. "I squeezed orange juice."

"Man, thank you, guys, so much," I tell them, going and making a plate and pouring coffee and orange juice and taking a seat at the table with all three of them.

"Can we work on our comic book today?" Jane asks.

And I tell her, of course, that I want to hang out just me and her all day.

The sun fills the kitchen.

There's a record playing—not old blues, but John Coltrane, an album called *Ascension.*

My dad talks about the book he's reading, and my mom talks about school and asks me how I feel about starting again on Monday.

"Good," I say—and that's the truth, though it'll be awkward seeing Eliza.

Still, I have my friends—Jackie and Preston and now Wanika. We've talked on the phone since we left the ward, and I'm actually gonna go get coffee with her in Berkeley tomorrow.

Not like in a romantic way—not at all. Just as friends. I need friends right now. And, as great as Preston is, he doesn't understand what it's like.

Wanika does.

And, to some extent, Jackie does, too. She struggles with her own . . . darkness? Something like that.

I have two real friends now. And I can talk to them about anything.

It's the shame and fucking secrets that will kill me. They almost did before. And they totally will again—if I'm not "rigorously honest," as they kept saying in treatment.

To tell the truth about who I am and what's going on with me, that is everything. Sharing. Asking for help. I gotta do that shit. I gotta try.

So I eat my breakfast with my family.

My mom, my dad, Jane.

We are all together.

Through everything.

And I have hope.

Real fucking hope.

That I can have a normal life.

And do all the things that normal people do.

If I just hold on.

And I don't let go.

EPILOGUE

JACKIE SITS ON THE concrete barrier wall with her legs hanging down.

The sun is bright and hot. The sky is a pale blue color.

The ocean surges. The waves crash down.

We both look out and say nothing for a long while.

There is something about watching the ocean—something pure and calming.

"It's beautiful," Jackie finally says.

And she's right. It is.

She takes off her hat and pushes her hair back. She leans on her elbows.

"There's a seal," she tells me, pointing.

I try to see it, but can't. In the sun, the scars across my wrists reflect white against the blue veins underneath. But they are healed now. And, with time, even the scars will fade.

"There it is," she says excitedly.

And this time I catch sight of it just as it ducks down beneath the surface of the water.

"Shark bait," I say.

Jackie laughs.

I take out a cigarette and light it and pass it over to Jackie, then I light one for myself.

I breathe in and out.

The world turns around me.

And, even these months later, most everything is status quo. Jackie and Preston are still together. Eliza and I still don't talk. My dad's still writing his book, working freelance. My mom's still in the Stanyan Hill library. Jane's still the greatest. And I'm still seeing Dr. Frankel twice a week.

I'm on that Clozaril. And it's working. It's all working.

For today.

"What time we meeting Preston at the Castro?" I ask.

She smiles. "Six." She swings her legs back and forth. "And Wanika's meeting us, too, huh?"

"Yeah," I say. "She is."

"How's she doing? She had any more . . . whatever you call 'ems?"

"No . . . I don't think so."

She smiles over at me. "What about you?"

"No. I don't think so."

She laughs. "Should we go then?"

"Yeah."

I stand.

And the ocean waves crash behind me.

ACKNOWLEDGMENTS

THANK YOU,

Jette Newell Sheff

My dad and Karen and Jasper and Daisy

And my mom

Amanda Urban

Kristen Pettit—this book owes everything to you

Hrishi Desai, Hrishi Desai, Hrishi Desai

Shari Goldhagen

Molly Atlas

Barrett Sheff

Mark, Jenny, Becca, Susan, Lucy, Steve

Nancy and Don

Charles Wallace

Nicole and Tim and Julian and Natalie and Cabbage and
    Matilda and all the birds

Kathy Sherrill

Johnny and Tomoka and Moera and John Wu

Armistead and Chris

Peggy Knickerbocker

Susan and Buddy

Dr. Larissa Mooney

Sue and Nan

Jenny and Jim and Heidi

Bo Feng

Yoko and Sean

Jerry Stahl, Jerry Stahl

Jeremy Kleiner

Brian Geffen

Michael Green

Max Gavron

Andre and Maria Jacquemetton

Powell Weaver

Jamison Monroe

Felix Van Groeningen

Leigh Redman

Shelly Zimmerman

Vin Nucatola

Cameron Crowe

Ramona Guitar Wolf Jackson

Rhett Butler

Cole the cat

Whoever owns that piece of land on Santa Monica
     Boulevard I sneak my dogs into, I'm sorry I keep
     cutting your fence

Love
N

ABOUT THE AUTHOR

NIC SHEFF is a columnist for *The Fix* and the author of two memoirs about his struggles with addiction, the *New York Times* bestselling *Tweak: Growing Up on Methamphetamines* and *We All Fall Down*. He also a wrote for the hit TV series *The Killing*. Nic lives in Los Angeles, California.

As a teenager and young adult Nic struggled with drug and alcohol addiction, as well as severe mental illness issues. His first two books were memoirs about his experience battling addiction. For his first novel, he wanted to examine what happens to someone who experiences the symptoms of schizophrenia while still a teenager, someone trying to manage the hardships of mental illness at such a fragile time of life—the everyday struggles of high school and relationships. Much of the novel is borrowed from his own experience, but it is also a departure. He hopes to show that mental illness is not a death sentence.